HANGING WATERS

HANGING WATERS

A NOVEL

by

KEITH WEST

Illustrated
by
NOEL SYERS

GRAHAM BRASH, SINGAPORE

This edition first published in 1990 by
Graham Brash (Pte) Ltd
227 Rangoon Road
Singapore 0812

ISBN 9971-49-207-5

Printed in the Republic of Singapore by
Chong Moh Offset Printing Pte. Ltd.

To
AH KAM

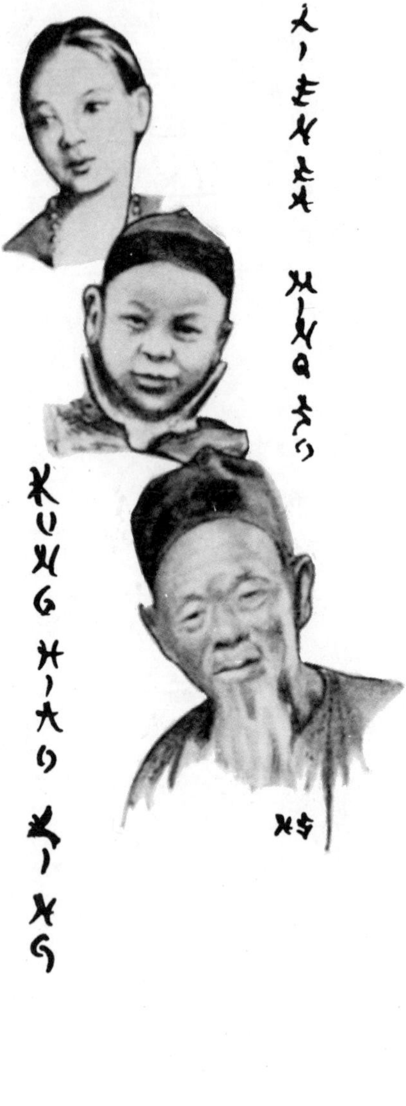
LIEN HUA
MING SO
KUNG HIAO KING
HS

CONTENTS

LIST OF ILLUSTRATIONS

Chapter I

UNCLE TUNG LAI LUK

" It is a pity," said Ming So, squatting on his heels on the raised embankment, " that the sides of this paddy-field are not in line with the points of the compass, for if they were we might expect a better yield of rice."

His mother halted the water-buffalo and gave a further roll up to each of her trouser-legs.

" What man told you that ? " she demanded. Then, without waiting for an answer, she raised one foot and splashed the water-buffalo. The signal moved the animal, the animal moved the wooden plough, and Ming Nai waded on across the paddy-field, the handles of the plough in her unswerving grip. Her son saw her turn at the far end. As she passed him again, she added, " Because he is no wiser than you are, my son." This time she did not even stop the plough as she passed.

Ming So remained squatting on the raised embankment which held the precious water in the paddy-field. By and by, to-morrow if not to-day, he would have to bucket water into that paddy-field – a work of considerable monotony, whose results were not immediately obvious. Therefore an unsatisfying piece of work. To-day, or to-morrow, or the week after – it did not matter much. His mother finished the few remaining mud-furrows, tethered the animal to a stake on the flat, raised bank, dragged the primitive plough to dry land, and came towards him.

" What man told you of the points of the compass ? " she demanded.

" It was Pai Kwat, the schoolmaster," Ming So told her as he rose to his feet and trotted along beside her, homewards. " He is a very great man, is Pai Kwat. He knows all that there is to learn of Feng Sui – the Science of Favourable Aspects – besides a great deal of other learning of which I have not plucked a single blade. He is a great man, is Pai Kwat. His voice tells his greatness to those who have the intelligence to observe. You have heard the booming note with which he instructs the children in the village school ? "

" Drums also boom, and drums are empty," said his mother succinctly. " No, my son, you are too ready to listen with attention to loud noises without duly considering their meaning. Of course, your dead father had the same fault, so that you probably inherit it from him. If your father had thought less of Feng Sui, in the matter of selecting his grave, there would be less need, now, for me to guide that foolish beast along uncounted furrows in our paddy-field. To buy land for his grave at the ridiculous rate which he paid for it, just because the land was supposed to be lucky ! Why, when men are dead, they all look the same." She laughed quietly to herself. "And smell the same, wherever their grave may chance to be," she added.

"But when people die," persisted the boy, "is it not of the highest importance where their graves may be? Does not the eternal comfort of the dead man's soul depend on the forethought which he or his family expend on the choice of a suitable burial-place? The honourable teacher, Pai Kwat, tells many tales of evil which has befallen a family because they did not pay due attention to Feng Sui."

Ming Nai snorted impatiently.

"Pai Kwat! Pai Kwat! Who is this Pai Kwat that his tales should deplete a widow's money-box? What does he know of anything except the over-praised wisdom of the ancients and the contents of his musty books? Now, if you ask me for the name of a wise man, I would mention your uncle, the honourable Tung Lai Luk, who is favouring our unworthy household with his presence to-day. There is a man for you, if you like! No nonsense about the tales of the ancients. Still, you have seen only thirteen winters, so that we must not yet expect from you the ripe judgment of your elders."

The boy skipped delightedly.

"To-day he is coming? I thought it was to-morrow." He left her side for a moment in fruitless pursuit of a water-rat. When the ripples of its dive had subsided, he returned. "And this great uncle of ours, why is he so great and wise a man? Has he learning, or money?"

" He possesses the learning which brings money, my son, and the money which that learning brings. He does not mistake to-day for to-morrow, nor noise for importance."

" I shall be very attentive when my uncle comes," said the boy. " It is possible to learn much by observation, and he must truly be a great man for you to say so." Thus he paid an almost unconscious tribute to his mother's critical faculties. " And I, who am the head of the family of Ming, have much need of knowledge if that family is to assume again its merited importance."

She said nothing to this, and presently they came to the small mud-walled house which was home. The poverty of the family had not prevented a certain neatness in the unambitious building : the two sleeping-rooms were as spotless as the one living-room, and even the kitchen at the rear exhibited an order quite unusual in a Chinese kitchen. Yet, even so, Ming Nai was not satisfied. Having washed the mud of the paddy-field from her legs, she set about a last and largely superfluous sweeping of the tiled floor, while Ming So, slicing beans into a basin, reflected on the mixed blessing of an uncle's visit. This was his mother's brother, he mused. Why, then, should his mother strive to make the house appear cleaner than it ought to be ? His mother's brother would know, being a wise man, that this tidiness was abnormal. But then, he also would know, being a wise man, that women are happiest when they seem to achieve perfection in the ordinary course of their duties, claiming (silently, of course) praise for the presumed permanency of this uncomfortable and unreal state.

Ming So sliced beans, while his mother swept and garnished. And by and by a carrying-chair set down at the devil-stopper outside the door. He heard an uncomplimentary remark from one of the coolies who had borne the chair, comparing the smallness of the house with the expected tip from Uncle Tung Lai Luk. Then his uncle had arrived, and Ming So, as titular head of the household, had secreted the beans in a cupboard and was bowing with a dignity beyond his years in the middle of the living-room.

" This is an honour of which even my mother is not worthy," he was saying, " much less myself."

Tung Lai Luk, the very picture of a successful business man whose stocky, unimaginative form had thrust through difficulties and (possibly) dangers, stood smiling, as a visiting uncle should smile, at the dignified figure of his little nephew. Behind him a coolie had deposited two black, shiny suitcases. Tung's small black skull-cap, decorated with a button of the third order of Mandarins, to which he was not entitled, nodded as if to say that here was all he could possibly have hoped for or expected.

"I, myself, am unduly honoured," he said, as custom prescribes – albeit he used the phrase as if he were fully aware of its emptiness. " And your honourable mother ? " he demanded.

At the words Ming Nai came from the smaller bedroom. Her hair had been freshly braided, she wore her best pair of black trousers, and her hands were folded in front of her as she stood, head bowed, awaiting her brother's permission to speak. For Ming Nai, despite her very clear-sighted ideas on the relations between men and women, played a part because she sought from this brother of hers, whom she despised not a little as a pompous gas-bag, advancement for her only son, Ming So. It was possible that he might offer to take the boy away with him to the distant city, there to give him that opportunity for advancement which she herself could not hope to provide.

" You are well, my sister ? " asked Tung Lai Luk.

" As well as circumstances and the perpetual mud of the paddy-fields permit," she replied. " But I have no right to complain, possessing as I do a brother who honours our roof with a visit, and a son who will be able to perform the ancestral duties at the tombs of his fathers. But do you come into our home and treat it as your own," she added, remembering what she wanted from her brother.

The coolies brought in the suitcases and put them down, looking askance at the coin which the merchant proffered. Ming So moved a chair into what he wished to appear a more convenient position. Ming Nai retired to the kitchen.

.   .   .   .

Night had not so much surrounded the little house as engulfed it – night with its spaced jewels hung in the branches of the nearly invisible trees – while a faint wind stirred small rustles under the door and round the eaves of the house. Uncle Tung Lai Luk had been fed and was now sitting on a porcelain barrel at one side of the table, while at the other side little Ming So valiantly played host and his mother put in an edged word when opportunity offered.

" And now," said Tung Lai Luk, " now that the familiarity fitting and decent between relations has begun to displace the formality fitting and decent between newly-met relations, may I enquire, sister, what you mean to do with this young nephew of mine ? "

" Do with him ? " Ming Nai almost forgot, in her delight that the subject had at last come under discussion, the deference due to her brother. " Do with him ? What can I do with him ? My eyesight is yet sharp enough to see that, here in the little village of Ha Foo, there is no suitable occupation for a boy of thirteen summers, no path wherein he may profitably walk, no goal towards which he may profitably strive. There are but the poor paddy-fields which the honoured and lamented father of Ming So did not sell in order to provide for fitting obsequies. Behind the plough, after the wooden harrow, as the proverb says, birds may profit, but seldom men."

Tung Lai Luk nodded his head in comprehension,

passing without comment over his sister's too great outspokenness.

" I know," he agreed. " For some moons, now, I have been considering the future of the lad, so far as my weightier business matters have permitted, and as the result of this exercise of forethought I do not think, sister, that you overstate the effect on the mind of a sensible boy of the monotony, the depressingly small returns, of our deplorably elementary methods of rice-culture. The paddy-field is not a suitable place for your son, my sister, nor for my nephew."

Ming Nai nodded in her turn.

" Your wisdom is, as ever, the *wisdom of jade*, and I daily return thanks to the ancestors of the Ming family for having permitted my son to have so excellent an uncle." She felt more or less confident, now, that Tung Lai Luk would make some proposal or other about the boy. " It is generous of you to spare the time to consider his plight."

" He is an intelligent boy," said Tung Lai Luk. " I presume that he has duly studied the classics – that he knows by heart the words of the Master, Confucius ? "

" His teacher, the honourable Pai Kwat, has often spoken of the progress which the boy has been making," assented Ming Nai, without specifying the matter of Pai Kwat's remarks.

Her brother did not misunderstand her, however. " We must remember that even learning may be deceptive," he said. " The wisest often impress their teachers little. Now, I have a proposition to make."

Ming Nai leaned forward. The moment for which she had been waiting had arrived. Ming So opened his mouth in apparent surprise, as his mother had told him to do whenever his mother nudged him with her foot.

Tung Lai Luk drew his chair slightly nearer to the chairs of Ming Nai and Ming So.

Chapter II

MOTHER-WISDOM

" Opportunities should be embraced with both hands," began Tung Lai Luk sententiously. " Now, in this land of paddy-fields there are few opportunities to embrace, and, if there are few opportunities, it is not to be expected that a boy like my nephew should prosper as is his undoubted right." He paused. " In the city, however, it is different. There, we find men of all sorts, and opportunities as many and as varied as the men. Do you not agree with me, my sister ? "

Ming Nai saw that, given time, he would come to the point, so she said : " You are as right as may be."

Thus flattered, Tung proceeded : " It is impossible for him to go to the city without having a position to which to proceed. I very much doubt if the gains which you, my sister, wrest from an unkind and reluctant land would provide enough funds to keep the boy in Kwei Sek for a single week. Therefore we must consider how a position for him may be found."

Ming So nodded at his uncle's wisdom.

" It is only the opportunity which is necessary," he said. " Given the opportunity, I should find little difficulty in taking due advantage of it."

" Do not be too confident," replied his uncle.

" It is one thing to have a plan and quite another thing to put that plan into execution. Now the plan which I have formed for you (after much consideration – and, I may say, much misgiving) necessitates an application, an industry on your part which you will find difficult of attainment. Remember that work, really hard work, is not always as pleasant as sitting on the banks of a paddy-field ; that to rise with the sun and go again to rest long after the sun's setting, calls for determination in one who has seen thirteen winters only. Remember that."

" I will do my best," answered the boy, not particularly depressed at the thought of the life of toil suggested by his uncle's words. He was trying to imagine what might be the nature of the promised opportunity. In his uncle's office ? A clerk ? Surely not. What then ?

" He is a good boy at times," ventured his mother guardedly.

Tung Lai Luk heaved the sigh of a man whose breast is full of important matters.

" I will take him into my house," he said. " Of course, at his tender age he can expect to receive only his food : I will, however, add to that some small money for such foolishnesses as boys are accustomed to find desirable. You, my sister, will doubtless be able and ready to provide him with a sufficiency of clothes to equip him for residence in such a household as mine."

" Clothes are unbelievably expensive," returned

Ming Nai. " Nevertheless, I will make an effort to provide him with what may be needful. For, indeed, so generous and unexpected an offer calls for me, in my turn, to do something for the boy. We are grateful, he and I, and I hope that you, my honourable brother, will not fail to understand how grateful we are." At the back of her mind she was thinking that the old miser might at least have given the boy his clothes. It would mean skimping and saving on her part for many moons before she could pay off the money which she would have to borrow in order to pay for those clothes. Still, even a single grain of rice was better than an empty rice-bowl. " I will do what I can."

The boy's delight at the prospect was in danger of overcoming the reserve which he knew to be expected of him.

" I am to go to the city with you, my uncle ? Oh, but that will be wonderful ! To see all the great men and learn how they make their money . . ."

"Do not expect too much of the city," said Tung, with unexpected wisdom. " It is, in many evil respects, very like the country in which you have been brought up." But the boy had not heard him : in imagination he was already amongst the great ones of the earth, learning how the elusive copper *cash* might be enticed towards the hand, like trout in a mountain stream. . . . Only in his imagination these copper *cash* had been transmuted to silver dollars, large, tinkling silver dollars.

" When do I go ? " he cried, and his mother answered him.

" In no such indecent and discourteous haste as you seem to desire," she said. " Run away now, and see that the back door into the kitchen is locked. I fear that I forgot it in the excitement of your honourable uncle's summons to speak with him on this matter of your future." When the boy had gone out of the room, she leaned over and whispered : " Can you not lend me the money for his clothes, at whatever rate of interest you may think right and just ? The moneylenders in this village of Ha Foo devour the very bones of those who are unlucky enough to need to borrow money from them."

" It has been a bad year," her brother replied. " Only the duty which I feel towards my family and their requirements gives me strength enough to keep on working, working, for a mere pittance. And you, who are not any longer of the family of Tung, having married the late lamented Ming Cheung Wai, should by rights depend on the family of the Mings for your aid in such a matter as this of clothing the lad. Still . . . I will buy clothes for the boy when he gets there ; you and he may regard it as a loan, to be repaid without interest as soon as the boy earns his money. I cannot take interest from you, even if we are now of different families. Ah, little nephew, and was the door locked ? " For the boy had come in again. " Your feet are silent on this rattan matting : I hope that one day your step will be more clearly audible when you enter. Thick paper soles on the polished boards, as marks a man of property." For he was feeling kindly towards the boy and to his sister Ming Nai, as benefactors always feel towards the objects of their benefactions.

His mother spoke for Ming So. " I trust, I also, that he may succeed. As the Master, Confucius, says, ' First cut and then polish,' and I hope that I have cut the jade well enough for you to polish it. Then indeed he may attain those heights of success which your words call up to me." She paused, wondering if this were precisely the right moment in which to press her brother for further concessions, then decided to venture. " But while, under your vigilant eye, he is gaining wisdom in the city, I am wondering who will assist me in the yearly duties of rice-planting here in Ha Foo. At present I have been able to snatch a bare subsistence from the reluctant soil : without Ah So I fear that even my increased efforts will be insufficient to bring in enough money to support me. And it would not be fitting that men should say of the widow of Ming Cheung Wai that she could not provide enough food for her brother when he condescended to visit her."

Tung Lai Luk was grave as he sat there.

" My sister, it is very unfortunate, but the clothes which I have promised and the food which this unproductive nephew of mine will consume represent the extreme limit to which I can stretch the purse of liberality. It has been a bad year, as I said : I have suffered losses : creditors are pressing, debtors reluctant. I am not as young as I was, and the strain is very heavy." His catalogue of woes exhausted itself. " No – I fear that what you ask is quite impossible."

Ming Nai nodded sagely as he ceased speaking. " That is all very true," she said. " It is as true of me as it is of you. But my suggestion (if I may be so bold as to make a suggestion) would be, I fancy, of advantage to us both."

" Go on : I am listening," said Tung Lai Luk.

" If I could have a *mui-tsai*, matters would right themselves," she proceeded. " Now I have not the money to buy one of these girls, nor (I believe) can you spare the money from your business in the city. Nevertheless Pai Kwat, the school-teacher, has ten children, and in the middle of the row-of-decreasing-size stands a daughter whose age is eleven summers. In a village such as this Ha Foo, Pai Kwat has little or no chance of marrying off this daughter of his." She turned to her son. " Run away again, Ah So, and stop away." They both waited until the boy had gone out. " Now, the family of Pai is an ancient family, and he would wish to marry the girl into a family of equal age, such as the Mings."

" I see," her brother nodded. " You propose to marry the two now. But the expense of a marriage such as befits the two families . . ."

" I do not propose to marry them now. I am

aware that in unenlightened parts of the Flowery Kingdom these marriages of children still happen, but I should regard it as a failure of my duty if I allowed my son Ah So to marry before he knew and appreciated the main purpose and at the same time the main disadvantage of marriage – the production of children. Long hours in the fields provide me with many thoughts which are all the better for an airing, so do not be shocked, my brother, if I appear outspoken."

" Go on," Tung returned, seeing no other course. " And what then do you propose ? "

" I propose that Pai Mei, the girl in question, should come to me until such time as Ah So, under your skilful tutelage, becomes capable of earning enough money to support a wife, whom he will then be able to treat as a wife expects to be treated. You will, I hope, talk this subject over with the learned Pai Kwat ; you will convince him, and you and I will sign a document to that effect. Thus I shall gain what is in reality a *mui-tsai*, while Pai Kwat will be free from the cost of the girl's food (which greatly troubles him) and will gain the promise of marriage into the ancient family of Ming. What say you, my brother ? "

" The proposal has less in it of folly than one would expect," conceded the other. " I will think it over, and if I agree I will see this Pai Kwat to-morrow morning. For the moment I am tired after much journeying."

She rose to her feet. " I fear that I have neglected my duties," she said. " I should have thought of that. May I show you the bed which I have put up for you ? . . ."

Their voices faded into a murmur. Ming So cautiously put his head round the corner of the door, made sure that the coast was clear, and then ran silently to the back door, closing it after him with considerable care.

Chapter III

IDYLL

At the back of the mud-walled house attached to the village school was a sleeping-room built on at a later date, designed to accommodate the overflow of the family which the generosity of the gods had given Pai Kwat, holder of the Hanlin degree and largely unpaid teacher to the horde of other children which the same liberal gods had rained upon the wedded couples of Ha Foo. The back wall of this additional room possessed a cracked and leaky oiled-paper window, and through the corner of this window, a long, thin twig of bamboo might be pushed with the accuracy of long practice, so that it would tickle the face of Pai Mei, sleeping there alongside four others of her family, tickle her face and awaken her without waking the others.

Only Ming So had the ability and practice to manœuvre the bamboo twig in this manner. Besides, he alone judged it to be worth while to run the risk of a beating from the schoolmaster Pai Kwat for the sake of a midnight meeting with Pai Kwat's daughter.

She came out now, after he had endured a little breathless wait in the shade of the bamboo-clump, and they moved out of sight (had any but the great, warm moon been looking), out of sight down the

path to their secret meeting-place in the malo-
dorous centre of what was at once the village rub-
bish-depository and the local breeding-ground for
mosquitoes.

He was thirteen : she was eleven. They stood
shyly looking at each other – they were always shy
for the first minute – and then Ming So said : " Let
us sit down here, on this log of wood, for I have much
to tell you which concerns us both. I am going to
the city with my uncle."

" That will be lovely," he heard the little voice
beside him whisper. Then came a suppressed
snuffling. " I am very glad," she sniffed.

" But you are weeping, Ah Mei ! " The boy was
astonished. " Why should you weep ? But listen :
there is other news besides that. You are to go to
the house of my honourable mother, to help her in
the fields, until I am old enough to return from the
city and marry you. Is not that wonderful ? The
thing which we had hoped has fallen on us like a
shooting star."

" But we shall not see each other any more – not
for many moons, at the very least," she wailed.
"Ooh! And I had found a new place where we
may go into the forest and bathe in the brook, and
I have caught a new *cicada* for you, a beautiful
cicada, the biggest I have ever seen, and it was going
to be a present for you, and – ooh ! "

The Chinese do not, as a rule, kiss. It is bad
manners, to say the least of it, thus to touch another

human being unnecessarily. Yet in the luminous night these two children sat side by side with their arms round each other, comforting, comforted. In the great black shadows under the high trees the metallic note of a *cicada* rang out shrilly, and in the wet mud by their feet a bull-frog belled.

" Little Star, my sweetheart, do not mourn," said Ming So. " It will not be for long, and think how wonderful it will be when I come back to marry you."

" You will find some other girl, and I shall pull her hair out, so that she shall be ugly and you will then come back to me," said Pai Mei, with determination and despair at once in her voice. " But how do you know, Ah So, that you will go away to the city ? "

" My uncle from Kwei Sek came to see us, as I told you that he would come, and he and my hon-ourable mother have been burning the oil while they sat and talked about me. I listened at the door, of course. They had sent me out, you see, because they wished to speak privately, though why they should wish to hide from me what is to happen to me, I cannot imagine. Now my mother will be looking for me, and I shall be beaten, and she will say that I am an evil child and a child of the evil spirits of the hillside. But it does not matter, Little Star." For she was crying again. " Take comfort. Come : we will forget my mother and your mother, and we will go to the new place in the forest which you say that you have found, and when

we come back, what will be, will be. Come, Little
Star, show me the place of which you spoke."

She stifled her sobs now, as she took him past the
high, hump-backed bridge with the stream roaring
underneath to fall into the back abyss below the
big tree, past the little shop of the leather-worker,
whose window still showed industrious light, and
down the narrow grass path beside the bottom
paddy-field. Then she turned to the right between
the bushes growing at the very corner of the field,
where the forest began.

And now, in the faintest of light, under the great
creepers brushing their faces, she led him through
the forest. Neither considered any risk which they
might be running, though some large animal moved
stealthily in the night and the path was difficult and
tortuous. Ever, ahead of them, sounded the roar
of a waterfall, and it was below this waterfall that
they eventually emerged, very close to each other,
into a gloom which seemed like daylight after the
blackness of the forest. Before them shone the water
of a pool which narrowed towards the end remote
from the fall, narrowed and became shallower, on
a gravel bottom. The ripples from the fall rushed
endlessly over the gravel and lost themselves in the
rank rushes of the bank.

" There ! " whispered Pai Mei, with almost the
pride of a landscape gardener. " Is it not lovely ? "

" It is a beautiful pool," agreed the boy. " And
the gravel here would be pleasant and clean for

the feet. But I have just remembered that, if I bathe now in these clothes, they will not be dry by the time I reach home, and in the absence of rain my mother will know what I have been doing. Also, when she consults with your own honourable mother to-morrow, she will find that you, too, returned home at a late hour in wet clothes and . . ."

" I can dry mine at the stove," said Pai Mei. " Besides . . ."

" What? And have you such a number of clothes, O affluent one, that you can afford to take out a clean suit to sleep in while the other dries? "

She put her arm round him.

" Let us bathe without," she whispered.

.   .   .   .

The moon had risen so far in the sky that at last her slanting finger touched the verge of the pool, then the pool itself. And in the pool, still very close to each other, stood Ming So and Pai Mei, little statues of grey-olive in the silver light. The water rippled round their ankles, and they cast a little ring of splashes with each movement, as water dripped from them.

" I wonder what my mother meant this evening when she spoke of treating a wife as a wife should expect to be treated? " Ah So was saying. " Little sweetheart, do I treat you as you would expect? "

" Yes," she whispered, and her arm tightened round him. Then, suddenly, " Ooh! We're in

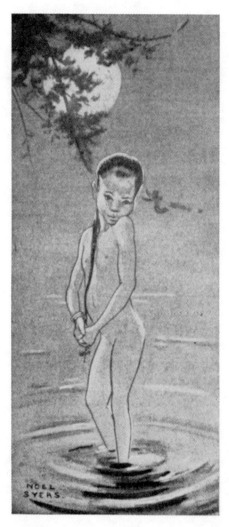

*" Let us
bathe without,"*
she whispered

the light ! " She let him go and dashed to the shore. Shortly afterwards, two completely naked children, each holding a parcel of clothes to be put on when their skins were dry, trotted homewards through the black tunnel of the forest.

On the forest's edge they dressed shyly, turning their backs on each other, then crept towards the village. At the bridge they parted, not lengthily, for each sensed danger from an angered parent.

And, indeed, at almost the same time shortly afterwards, two irate mothers were engaged in chastising their children, so that two shrill cryings disturbed the night.

Ming So yelled because he wanted to make his mother think that she had hurt him enough. Besides, it would wake up Uncle Tung Lai Luk, and then his mother would stop beating him.

But Pai Mei cried much more bitterly than her mother's blows warranted, because Ming So was soon to go away to the city.

Chapter IV

THE SORCERER

On the ceiling swung slowly the pattern of light which escaped through the triangular holes in the brass cover of the little hanging lamp. This pattern of yellow points circled about the hook from which the lamp depended by its length of brass chain : the brass oil-container threw a deep cone of shadow below the lamp. In the four corners of the room tiny pin-pricks of red smouldered steadily in the darkness, and four invisible coils of scented smoke rose upwards from the glowing *heung* which had been lit there. The whole room was filled with the overpowering sweetness of this incense, so that to the man sitting motionless in the cone of blackness it seemed as if the slowly circling pattern of light above him were receding upwards, outwards, to the infinite heavens, leaving him seated at the hub of the world, while about him the stars turned for ever in their slow paths.

Before him lay, open, the *I-Ching* – the Book of Changes – at the seventeenth hexagram, and, although he could not see the book, he was now repeating aloud, like an incantation, the meaning of the sixth line in the hexagram :

" The sixth line, undivided, tells us to look at the whole course that is trodden, to examine the presage which that gives. If it be complete and without failure, there will be great good fortune."

His voice ceased as the lamp chain reached the limit of its torsion, and the stars halted and began to retrace their unhurried paths in the drugged heavens.

" To consider the future of which it tells," repeated Pai Kwat : " to consider the future . . ."

He lifted the cover of a chased brass incense-burner standing beside him, and threw on the glowing sandalwood a pinch of powder. To the sweetness of *heung* was now added a bitterness as of the rough taste of an unripe orange.

" To consider the future. . ." murmured Pai Kwat: " to consider the future. . . ."

In the darkness into which he stared hung the face of his daughter, Pai Mei, and beside her face another dimly showed – Ming So's face, turned towards the girl.

" The plain ground for the colours," quoted Pai Kwat sonorously from one of the passages of the Master, Confucius, which he did not quite understand. " Yes – I have considered the future. It shall be so."

He rose to his feet a little unsteadily and went out of the room towards his bed, while behind him in the empty room the pale yellow stars of light still circled endlessly, retraced endlessly their tireless orbits, and four red glow-worms in the corners of the room showed faintly in an atmosphere mingled of sweet and bitter.

Cw

Chapter V

A BARGAIN

The arrival of Pai Kwat at the house of the Mings was a matter for no little ceremony ; little Ming So, during school-time, had never treated his teacher with the deference which now, on all hands, that august personage found prepared against his visit. But, then, the boy was able to reflect, Chinese customs clothe the aged with a dignity which the profession of school-teacher is liable to destroy, and here Pai Kwat was no longer striving to instil into effervescent childhood the meaning of the more recondite passages of the Chinese classics. No – not at all. Pai Kwat was here as the father of Pai Mei, and in this capacity he had come to discuss with Uncle Tung Lai Luk the proposal for his daughter's future. Dignity was therefore fitting. But it was amusing to see them together – the old and the new. Pai Kwat would quote some doubtless relevant passage from a book which Tung had forgotten (or never read), and Tung would reply gravely with the wisdom of the merchant, always countering theory with practice and wisdom with money. They were talking now.

" *A wise man adapts himself to circumstances, as water fits the jar,*" said the old man. " I have little money, and the security of my small daughter necessitates a certain amount of forethought on my part. *Diseases may be cured, but not destiny.*"

"What you have said is wise, and indeed where should we expect to find wisdom, if not in our teachers?" agreed Tung Lai Luk. "It clearly behoves us parents and guardians, therefore, to see that Nature's bounty is not wasted, and in what way, I ask you, could that better be managed than by a formal contract between your honourable daughter and my sister's unworthy son?" He spoke thus deprecatingly of his nephew in consonance with immemorial belittlement. "In a few years he will, doubtless, have gained in wisdom and ability, so that, by the time that the family peach is ripe, he will make her a husband no more useless than most husbands are."

The teacher nodded. "True," said he. "And yet it is an unusual thing for me to give my daughter to your sister as a help in the house. I have misgivings when I consider a course so uncharted in the ancient habit of our race, so unjustified by precedent."

"But think of the advantages!" urged the merchant, as if he were selling something. "You have no longer to support your daughter, to provide her food, her raiment. You will know that she is in a good family, where she will learn manners and the finer points of housekeeping. Thus your mind will be at rest, and her shrill voice will not any longer disturb your nightly studies. Her mother will be

freed from the responsibility of looking after her.
And, when the years have made my unworthy
nephew a man of importance and your daughter
a useful woman, the two houses will be united by
bonds which are firmer than mere words. We both
stand to gain not a little by my suggestion."

Ming Nai smiled where she sat, a little behind and
apart from the two men. That her brother should
thus claim credit for her own idea mattered naught,
if he could persuade old Pai Kwat of the desirability
of the proposed arrangement. Ming So, beside her,
listened with ill-concealed delight to each point
made by his uncle and with hardly veiled intolerance
when Pai Kwat, with warning forefinger, put forth
his absurd objections.

" *A gem must be ground by the polisher of gems, as man
must be perfected by adversity*," said Pai Kwat. " I do
not think that your promising nephew has yet had
his share of trouble. *It is only in winter that men know
the pine and the cypress to be evergreens.* They say that
the full stomach cannot understand hunger, and you
cannot deny that he has been housed, fed, and
tended better than the average boy has a right to
expect. But what efforts has he made to repay his
mother's devotion ? Is his work at my school such
as to lead me to expect the constant application, the
unceasing labour, necessary to make him into a
worthy citizen ? *A parent's affection is best shown by
teaching the child industry and self-denial.* But has the
boy worked ? Has he denied himself ? " He raised

his shoulders heavenwards, and Ming So, unobserved, made the motion of spitting. Having thus relieved himself, he listened again.

"But, sir," argued his uncle Tung, "*ivory is not obtained from a rat's teeth.* The boy is a good boy – he has aided his widowed mother for many a year. We cannot all shine at the purely intellectual pursuits of whose perfection you are so bright an example. Can you imagine a world filled with nothing but literary men? No, there are other virtues besides the virtue of attainment in letters. If we were all students of the ancient classics, who would plough the rice-fields?"

"That again is true," agreed Pai Kwat. "And yet I would have had the lad strive harder with his writing-brush. *Who swallows quickly chews but little*, they say, and despite my frequent reproofs the boy persists in a merely superficial, parrot-like learning of such poor matters as I can find to teach him." The speaker nodded as if to compliment himself for his sagacity. "When he is compelled to support the wife whom now we propose to contract to him, he will have to make efforts far greater than those which he has hitherto made."

"May I suggest," Tung countered, "that they also say that *in a wife, virtue is needed, in a handmaid, beauty.* And we cast no aspersions on your family when we suggest that your daughter Mei is not outstandingly noted for one or the other. Yet we offer her marriage, in a year or two, with the eldest son, the only son, of an honourable family. Can you really hope to obtain for her a better offer elsewhere ? "

" I would not have you imagine, for a moment," protested Pai Kwat, " that I underestimate in any way the honour which you propose to do to my humble family. No. But to a father the responsibility for a daughter is nearly as great as the responsibility for a son, and while I perhaps strive *to add legs to the snake* in thus discussing the proposition further, I know that you will attribute my prolixity to the love which I bear my daughter, not to any failure to measure fairly the honour of your suggestion."

" Then it is settled ? " The merchant strove to clinch the bargain.

" Settled ? I thought we had only just begun to discuss it," said Pai Kwat, with raised eyebrows. " Now, as to money . . ."

" *You cannot strip two skins from one cow*," said Tung Lai Luk, very hastily.

" True. But *to swim with one foot on the ground* is a mark of prudence in the learner. And money, that evil necessity, cannot with impunity be ignored. You propose to contract my daughter to your nephew. How much would you . . . ? "

" My family is poor," said Tung. " We have difficulty in filling our own rice bowls, let alone those of others. Besides, is not the advantage of taking one mouth from your table a matter of money ? "

"She does not eat much," suggested Pai Kwat hopefully. "To split a melon-seed in thus calculating is a feat beyond my powers. No : some more definite payment – some tangible consideration . . ."

Ming So could contain himself no longer.

"But I love Pai Mei," he cried. "What is all this talk of money?"

His mother seized him by the ear. "Little chatterbox!" she cried. "You will go in here, in the kitchen, and stay there, silent, while wiser people discuss things which really matter. Love, indeed! And how can love fill the rice-bowl? Can love buy clothing? In here, silent, then." She shut the door on the boy, and, returning, lowered her head in seeming respect as she again took her seat somewhat apart from the two men.

"You see with what feather-brained notions his head is full!" said Pai Kwat. "I feel more strongly than ever that I should be doing definite wrong if I contracted my daughter to your nephew without some bond more lasting than the love of which the boy prattles."

"*He who does not soar high will suffer the less by a fall,*" said Tung Lai Luk. "So you propose? . . ."

. . . .

Later on, when Pai Kwat had gone, Ming Nai said to her brother : "The old fool desired the contract as heartily as we desired it. Why need he make such an ado about the money?" She knew the answer to this question before Tung Lai Luk spoke.

" Great wealth comes by destiny, moderate wealth by industry. Pai Kwat is a very industrious man," he replied. " And, now that all is signed, we shall make arrangements for my return to the city, with your son, the day after to-morrow. I must interview the coolies about the baggage." He went out.

" Pai Mei will be here for one day before I go ? " said the boy to his mother. " That will be lovely. And may we go out together for a little while ? There is much to say when a man and a woman part."

His mother smiled tolerantly.

" As you will, my son. You will soon have to decide things for yourself without my help, so you may start now. But, first, there is the wood which you promised to fetch for the fire."

Ming So sighed.

Chapter VI

THE TEMPLE OF MEMORY

" Yes, all is prepared for the journey," said Ming So. " My clothes are all packed in the shiny black boxes, and there is nothing more to be done."

Pai Mei regarded him tearfully, for even at eleven years she knew that there was something of finality about this parting.

" For many years I shall not see you," she said, and her eyes were wet. " Here, in Ha Foo, I shall be serving your mother and doing, probably more thoroughly than you ever did, the things which she demands of me. I shall help her in the duties of the house : I shall help her in the paddy-field. And while I am here, where nothing ever happens, you will be very far away in the great city on the river to the east, occupied with countless matters of business, meeting countless people, and thinking not at all of me."

" Sweetheart," the boy assured her, " I shall always think of you. When, at night, I look out above the busy housetops to see the *moth's eyebrow* moon resting on a silver cloud, I shall think that you will be looking, perhaps, at the same moon. Over the dark trees you will see the moon and think of me. I shall go to bed each night thinking of you, and, though we shall have between us more journeying than a strong horse could encompass in days, yet in our dreams we shall be together. There are always dreams."

" They say," whispered the girl as she trotted up the path beside him, " that my honourable father knows how to reconcile the opposing principles of the *ying* and the *yang*, that he can foretell the future and see the hidden metal which lives deep in the hearts of the mountains. They say that he has control over the spirits of the upper air, and that each night, when he retires to his room with his books, he travels far on the sure back of a moonbeam. I do not know much of such things, but I shall try to learn his arts, whereby a man may ride on a moonbeam from place to place."

" Why should you do this ? " Ming So demanded. " Only two or maybe three days past I was learning in school that chapter of the works of the Master, Confucius, which tells us that *study of the supernatural is harmful*. How can your honourable father teach us these words of the Master and then, each night, ride on the back of a moonbeam ? A coat cannot be both black and white, nor ground both wet and dry at once."

" Yes – a coat may be made of two kinds of cloth," she replied, " and ground may be damp in one place, wet in another, and dry in a third. But it does not matter : I *know* that my honourable father can do these things, and I shall strive to learn from him how they may be done."

" Why ? " insisted the boy. " Why do what the Master says is dangerous ? "

" And have you known so little of women that you do not understand ? I shall learn in order that I, too, may pass in the night over the silver and black fields of the sleeping earth towards the city where you also will be slumbering. I shall come to you when you do not expect it." She looked up at him with a sudden fear. " You do not *really* mind, do you ? I will only do it if you wish it, for I am to be your wife, and I would not wish to disobey my husband."

" I ? I mind your travels on a moonbeam ? Oh, no ; for I do not believe all these tales of strange magic. Such things do not truly happen. Men talk, and then women talk, and a tale is born. You may do as you will, little one. But remember that, if my mother makes you work too hard, you can always run away and come to me in the city. I shall soon be a great man, so that there will be much space in my house. And my mother keeps her money hidden in the bottom drawer of the medicine-cupboard, in a package on which is written ' Powdered Snakeskin.' You have only to take what you need for the journey, and, when you come, I will send back to my mother the money which you have taken."

" But I have seen my father riding on a moonbeam," persisted Pai Mei.

" It was a cloud of an unusual shape, which the

gods sent to deceive you," replied Ming So. " Now, do you understand what you are to do if my mother treats you ill ? "

The girl nodded. The path up which they were climbing wound between the great eucalyptus-trees and rank undergrowth towards the summit of the hill. Below, to one turning back, the village of Ha Foo might be seen nestling amongst the green like a dusty red flower. In front of them a single tall pagoda pointed immovably at the sky, and even now, at this distance, the two children could hear faintly the tinkle of the wind-bells suspended from the eaves of this pagoda.

" We shall soon reach there," Ming So told her. " Then we shall kneel before the golden image of the enlightened Buddha, asking for a blessing on our promise to each other."

" Can the Buddha really help ? " she asked. Then she said nothing more for a while. Deep in the forest on either hand could be heard rustlings, movings, in the gloom beneath the great trees, and Pai Mei was just a little frightened. When Ah So had gone away with his uncle to the city, she would have to walk up this path alone, to kneel alone before the golden Buddha and watch the strange face above her, wreathed in the smoke of incense.

" It was not a cloud," she said suddenly. " Because I saw him move to a more comfortable position, and you could not do that on a cloud. It was a moonbeam."

But now further discussion was forgotten, for they had emerged into the public courtyard. A yellow-robed priest with shaven head glanced incuriously at the two children as they crossed the courtyard and entered the shrine.

The long, low room was empty save for these two and the great golden presence of the image. Up the pink wood pillars writhed carven dragons whose heads were lost in the canopy of drifting smoke. Before the image were set small bowls of rice, and a tray of smouldering powder in a long train, arranged like one of the intricate Chinese characters on the seal of Pai Kwat, the schoolmaster. . . . The two knelt. From behind them a breath of wind blew, cooling the back of the neck. Somewhere in the interior of the building a voice sounded faintly, reciting a chapter from the Diamond Sutra.

" *To be and yet not to be,*"

intoned the hidden voice.

> " *To be and yet not to be,*
> *Together, at the same time,*
> *Endlessly.*
> *To be and yet not to be. . . .*"

Pai Mei sobbed quietly as she knelt there. Ming So was reflecting that, in the city, there would be many other things to do besides kneeling before images of Buddha. And, after all, these religious ceremonies were meant for women rather than for men. . . .

They each dropped a copper *cash* into the great bronze bowl at the entrance of the shrine.

" I shall come here often," said the girl. " It is very lonely on the path climbing through the forest, but I shall come."

" They say that a man may make, in the city, enough money in a single week to live in Ha Foo for a whole year," said Ming So. " I shall soon be very rich."

" You will not forget me ? " she whispered. " In the city there are many strange women, much more beautiful women than I, and it is very easy for a man to forget what he has promised."

" I shall not forget. Of course I shall not forget," he cried scornfully. " I have promised. And, besides, these strange women of whom you have been speaking are doubtless a great expense, and I desire to make and save money rapidly. No, assuredly you may rest content about that. Women are all very well in their place, but when a man sets out to become rich . . ."

But Pai Mei was not listening at all. In imagination she was climbing on a moonbeam which would shortly deliver her, breathless from the speed of its motion, in a room in the city where Ming So would be sitting talking to a strange woman. And then . . .

Chapter VII

BORROWED PHILOSOPHY OF A POET

" During my own youth," said the voice of Uncle
Tung Lai Luk from the closed carrying-chair, " I
could walk for many miles without becoming tired.
To rise in the morning with the punctual birds, to
work while light lasts, and then to sleep the sound,
dreamless sleep of a healthy boy – that was the
ancient way. Now our youth has apparently become so effeminate that a walk like this, beside my
chair, brings fatigue before twenty *li* have been
covered. What would you, Ming ? That I should
descend from my chair into the rain and give my
place to you ? Are there not bearers for your meagre
luggage ? Have you not the burden only of your
own body ? " The voice died away in grumblings.
It seemed a less jolly uncle who now spoke to the
boy from the comparative comfort behind those
green blinds of oiled cloth.

" I did not complain, Uncle Tung," said the
boy. " I said that I was tired – I did not complain.
And as for your descending from the chair, quite
apart from the question of the rain, I think that
would be foolish, since it is improbable that you
could walk so fast or so far as these coolies who bear
your chair on their shoulders, or even as I, who plod
along beside you in the mud."

From within the closed chair came the sound of a match being struck, then a wisp of smoke from a cigarette.

" Let us hear no more, then, of this tiredness of yours," said his uncle. " It is foolish to repine over things that are past, and our journey, or this part of it, is almost over. Through the holes in the front blind I can already see the red roofs of Ch'ang Sui, and at Ch'ang Sui a boat awaits us. Then your shoe-leather will have less work to do. Three days lying on your back in a boat, with nothing whatever to occupy you. Is that more to your taste ? "

" I do not know," answered the boy, " until I have experienced the leisure of which you speak. Never in my life have I lain on my back for three days, and I cannot foretell what my feelings will be. Is the country through which we shall pass on this boat as interesting as the country at Ha Foo ? Are there hills, valleys, and rice-fields, waterfalls and bridges ? " He was remembering his expeditions with Pai Mei, who was now presumably labouring with his mother in the fields.

" All country is interesting, if a man has not seen it before and is prepared to make the effort needful in order to be interested," said Tung Lai Luk. " But I think that the rain has stopped. The coolies may roll up the blinds again."

.   .   .   .

The river at Ch'ang Sui offers to the uninitiated little promise of navigation. The stream runs purling over rapids on one side of the river, while on the other a deeper stretch of water laps against the primitive bamboo wharfs as if it merely needed a flood to sweep away those flimsy structures down towards the distant sea. But when the Spring rains have passed and the river has sunk again into comparative tranquillity, passage boats come and go, and the little village of Ch'ang Sui wakes from sleep, to become the centre of transport for the whole province.

" The river is very swift," said Ming So, regarding it. " And although I can understand how one may go down the river, how is it possible to return ? "

" It requires many men and much rope to pull a boat up the swifter portions of the river," agreed his uncle, as he stepped aboard. " But ours is the easier journey. It merely needs a watchful steersman. Nature does the rest, like the good servant she is. Come : bestow your goods here, under this rattan awning. The crew sleep under that other awning in the bows. You may be thankful, my nephew, that you are not travelling on a public boat, where space is limited and the most ordinary privacies are neglected. I have hired this boat because I cannot endure to have strangers treading on my feet and interfering with my comforts. That is the reward of toil, my nephew : to have enough money to ensure privacy, at all events. See – the
Dw

boat-master is casting off the straw ropes which hold us to the wharf. The journey is about to begin."

He sat down, cross-legged, on the mat. The bow of the boat swung out into the stream, then round, and when a last push had been given from the bank, the view of the red roofs and flimsy wharfs of the little village of Ch'ang Sui fell astern. The steersman, feet braced on the deck, manœuvred his great steering-oar : the chatter of the wharf died away, to be succeeded by the continuous rustle of waters past the hull and the occasional roar of shallow water over rocks. A bend in the river obscured Ch'ang Sui. On each side stretched green forest, hills, mighty trees, and ever the boat seemed to shoot down through the smoother, deeper water, avoiding the rocks as by a miracle.

" I still marvel," said Ming So, " at the exceeding swiftness of the stream. Surely men cannot haul a boat up-river against the force of the current ? "

" They can do so. Obviously they do not build a new boat every time they desire to go down ! But if I had not come up-river myself, I should have been reluctant to believe in the possibility of it." Tung Lai Luk laughed. " You remind me of that poem of Li Tai Po. I trust that you have at least heard of Li Tai Po ? "

" His name I know – of his fame I am regrettably ignorant, my uncle. What was this poem ? Pai Kwat used to read poems to us at school, but I never remember having heard one written by this Li Tai Po."

" His poem – and he was a very famous poet – was written to the women of Pa, a village on the rapid head-waters of just such a river as this. It runs something thus : ' To the women of Pa. At Pa the river runs exceedingly swiftly, so that a boat travels a thousand *li* in a few days. How fortunate it is, O, women of Pa, that your husbands return to you upstream ! ' "

" That is a fine-sounding poem," agreed the boy. " But I do not wholly appreciate the meaning which it must possess. Why was Li Tai Po glad that the husbands of the women of Pa had to return upstream ? "

His uncle laughed again. " Li Tai Po was a man, like the rest of us, I suppose. He wrote the poem at Pa. There, no doubt, he found charming women – poets always find charming women. And presumably the husbands of these women were absent, on business, down the river. They would have to return, therefore, upstream, and the journey upstream was long and slow. So the poet Li Tai Po, writing his poems at Pa, would have the longer time in which to console those wives for the absence of their husbands – a very pleasant pastime, as all who have tried it with a pretty woman will tell you."

" But, uncle, I still do not wholly understand. For if these women were married, surely Li Tai Po would have nothing to do with them ? And a good woman would have nothing to do with a man who was not her husband, even if he was a very famous poet. So you see . . ."

" Oh, foolish boy ! Truly the Master said, ' *The careful people of the villages are the thieves of virtue.*' For you, coming from Ha Foo, think that people do always what they should, not what they desire. Thus you steal virtue for yourself, at the expense of those men, more men than you, who let the maxims of sages be conveniently forgotten, who put discretion behind them, when a bright eye calls, who willingly barter a little of your village approval for a night with a village girl whose husband is absent."

The boy brooded for a while, watching the bright sequence of the passing landscape. Then he said : " No doubt such are the habits of poets. But neither you nor I write poetry. Therefore no such excuse lies available for us."

" You have much to learn, my nephew. Now lie on your back on the matting and go to sleep, or at any rate cease your chatter, for I am tired." He arranged himself in comfort and closed his eyes. " Man is the servant not so much of his virtues as of his eyesight, where a pretty girl is concerned," he observed finally.

CHAPTER VIII

BOTTOM, THOU ART TRANSLATED

MING So suddenly woke up in the night and lay
perfectly still in his blanket. For a moment he
imagined himself back at his mother's house in Ha
Foo, and half listened for the familiar rustle of the
night wind in the clump of bamboos beside the gate.
But his ears now caught a very different rustle –
the sound of silk rubbing on silk. Then a voice
spoke on the deck near him – a woman's voice.

"There are many mouths to be fed in the village,
and little wherewith to feed them. Therefore, hearing of your arrival at the village of Seung So, I told
my friend here of the previous business which I did
with you a year past, suggesting that you might be
willing to take into your own rich household one of
these mouths. Her father has two sons and seven
daughters."

"Let her father speak for himself," said the voice
of Tung Lai Luk. "For always it is best, in affairs
of this sort, to deal directly between principals. Not
that I shall forget that you have performed the intro-
duction. Let him speak for himself."

"I am Yang Foo, a man of this village of Seung
So," said a third voice, on the invitation, and the
voice was the voice of an old man. "I have two
sons and seven daughters, as has been said. Last

year, as you must know, our crops were almost destroyed by blight, and all the weaving which has been from the immemorial past the duty of our women in the winter was finished a moon ago. Yet even that has brought a poor price in the market, and I have left but little money wherewith I may buy rice for myself and my family."

" Fortune is unkind," agreed Tung Lai Luk. " *But it is only in winter that we know the pine and the cypress to be evergreens.*"

" Then," the old man proceeded, " I have but one course open to me. Girls are of use in the winter weaving, but if there is no more of that weaving to be done, the head of a family becomes painfully aware that they have mouths, eating, eating, unproductively. Now a rich man like yourself can employ usefully in his house more women than I, who am only a poor man. A very poor man. If, in return for my daughter here, I might receive sufficient money to keep myself and my family until the harvest . . ."

" It is a pity that you did not come in daylight," said Tung Lai Luk. " But, since we arrived at dusk and leave at dawn, I suppose such a thing would have been impossible. Very well, man has made lanterns where the miserly gods refuse daylight. So let us look at this girl of yours." An arrow of light shot under the awning where Ming So lay, as a lantern was moved. " Why, but she is an ill-favoured little thing ! " Tung complained. " Even had your harvest been better, I doubt greatly whether you would have succeeded in finding the girl a husband. Though a man be concerned almost wholly with the cultivation of the fields, he would, I imagine, prefer to have a comely companion when those labours are over and he returns to the home roof-tree. But this daughter of yours . . ."

"My daughter is as her mother bore her," said the quavering voice. "I have heard, too, from my friends, that they consider her not unbeautiful. Nay, it is not seemly thus to belittle her in order to bring down the price. Come – there is no need to adopt commercial methods with me. I am her father, and a daughter is not a thing to be haggled and bargained over. Make me your offer, and, if it be reasonable, good. If not, good also. The gods have taken away our food – let the gods provide other food. The responsibility is theirs."

The woman's voice broke in. "Before you name prices," she said, "let us decide what proportion of this price I shall receive. For I have gone to much trouble and loss of time in order thus to arrange a meeting between you. What proportion?"

"Of every five *cash*, you shall have one and her father four," said Tung Lai Luk. "Now, is that to your liking?"

"It will serve, though it is not generous," the woman returned.

"Good. Now, I will make an offer. As I have said, she is not of the marrying sort, and it will be

difficult to find her a husband when she gets too old
to be useful to me. Still, we may find occupations
for her which do not too much depend on beauty.
Say a hundred and fifty dollars."

" You would not get a girl like that, a strong,
fine girl, for less than five hundred dollars," retorted
her father. " And you offer me a hundred and
fifty ! Come – there is no use in discoursing further.
I have been insulted. It is the price of but the foot
of a girl, not of her whole body. Come : we will go."

There was the sound of people rising to their feet.
Then the voice of the boy's uncle said soothingly :
" Nay – be not over-hasty. Maybe I have over-
looked some virtue in the girl. Sit down again."
The voices fell to a murmur.

Ming So was still tired, after his walk of the morning, and when he next woke there was silence on the
boat, except for the ripple of the still moving water
where it eddied past the piles of the bamboo pier and
rustled along the planking of the stationary boat.
Then his ears detected another sound, too – the
sound of dry, voiceless sobbing from the deck beside
him.

The boy lay for a while listening to these sounds.
In the sky, as he saw it through the open end of the
rattan awning, a faint promise of dawn showed. In
another hour the journey would begin again. Why
sacrifice that hour's sleep because some unhappy
person saw fit to weep in that particularly irritatingly
silent way just beside him ?

" Be quiet, or I will hit you ! " whispered Ming So, and then withdrew his own head under the protection of the blanket.

. . . .

Dawn had drawn aside her curtains of grey-silver and the great golden ball of day topped the hills in the distance ahead of them, down-river. Ashore, the village was already astir. Coolies staggered with their loads : a woman appeared for a moment at the door of a hut, charcoal sticks in her hand. In the bows of the boat a man turned over on his back, sighed in a long-drawn " Ai-ah ! " and sat up.

Ming So also sat up, to survey the world. Uncle Tung Lai Luk snored slightly at the rear of the shelter, where the draught was least. Rolled in his blankets, with only the profile of his sleeping face to be seen, he did not rouse in the boy any sentiments at all. Ming looked at his uncle exactly as he would have looked at a pile of clothing. But, sleeping in the entrance to the shelter, at the opposite side to the boy, lay the arrival of last night, in a cotton wrap somewhat too small to cover her completely. She had rolled the sides under her, so that she resembled a cylinder, from the end of which her feet protruded. Ming So studied these feet. They were, of course, unbound – for what would be the use in a labouring household of a girl crippled by foot-binding ? Strong, healthy feet they were, the toes parallel to each other, flattened somewhat by constant walking barefoot.

The toenails were short, bent over slightly towards the sole of the foot, and dirty.

She must be about fifteen, Ming decided : much older than Pai Mei, his sweetheart. Her flat little face looked unseeingly at the roof, for she was still asleep. Beside her, in a small bundle tied with a cloth strip, lay what he imagined were all her worldly goods. The girl's mouth was slightly open, and between the rather thick lips the boy could see part of a strong white set of teeth.

The crew were moving now. A rope was cast off. Someone shouted, and the steersman clambered round on the gunwale of the boat, leaning on their rattan shelter, as he made his way to the stern. At the sound of his passage the girl woke as Ming watched her.

He had never seen a girl wake up before. Of course, there was that time when Mei had gone to sleep at the edge of the paddy-field, in the long grass, and he had awakened her with a splash of cold water. But, then, that did not really count. Mei's awakening had been too sudden to compare with this.

The strange girl opened her eyes a little way, so little that he was not sure if she had opened them at all, then shut them again. A sort of wriggle passed down the grey cylinder in which she lay, and she made an effort to draw her feet into the warmth within. But so tightly was the cloth rolled about her that when she drew up her knees the encircling cloth cylinder followed. She opened her eyes again, wider this time. A puzzled expression crossed her face, and she looked round her with apparent interest. Then she sat up and unrolled herself in one movement, sitting in her cotton covering with her feet drawn under her, fully dressed.

" *T'so shan !* " said Ming So, in the universal greeting whereby men of every race assure each other that the morning, at all events, is good, whatever may be expected of the rest of the day. " Have you eaten your rice ? " For this latter question is also a politeness – however obvious the truthful answer may be. But somehow the very word " rice " reminded the girl of those economic reasons which had led to her being seated on the deck of a strange boat, now racing downstream, instead of facing an inadequate stock of food and an irate mother in her own house. She remembered the transaction of last night, and the separation from her parents and family which it implied. At any rate, Ming So concluded that this was so, since she began to cry again, softly, silently.

He rapidly put on the outer clothing which one discards on going to bed, folded his blankets in a neat pile, and went forward where the cook was engaged in coaxing a small charcoal brazier into a flame. As he went forward the boy made a slight detour and spat expressively into the river below. Why should women always be crying ? He spat again, then went on towards the cooking.

.   .   .   .

Breakfast in China is not an early meal, to be sniffed at before the appetite has properly grown to breakfast-point. It was, perhaps, half-past nine when Ming returned to the awning in the stern of the boat. He found it easy to sit, as he had been doing, in the bows and watch the wheeling landscape approach, pass, and fall astern of them, to gaze over the side at the undulating water and see in its turbid depths the occasional gleam of a polished rock over or past which the boat shot miraculously. And only the familiar smell of cooked food, which reached him on a sudden, erratic breath of wind, recalled him to appetite and its gratification.

The other two passengers were now sitting opposite to each other on the deck under the awning, eating. He noticed for the first time that his uncle's jaws and throat moved convulsively, and that as they did so they emitted a milder version of the noise which is made by a cow – a squishing, propelling noise. As he sat down and took from the girl the bowl containing his own ration of rice, he was displeased to find that his own eating, too, was not exactly silent. Further, the girl as well was making these faint, unpleasant sounds, which he had now noticed for the first time, as she ate her own rice. This amused the boy at the same time that it annoyed him, but he took longer than usual in finishing his first bowl, in the effort to achieve silence, only to discover that his uncle had, by then, removed to his own bowl the best of the dainties which lay in the steaming dish on the deck between them, for consumption and appreciation when the first bowl of rice should have dulled the edge of appetite.

" You slept well ? " Uncle Tung Lai Luk asked kindly.

" Oh, yes, uncle, except that early this morning I was awakened by strange noises from this girl. I was compelled to tell her to be quiet before I could recatch my sleep."

" We must excuse her," said his uncle. " She is a little sad just now, because she, too, is leaving her home to experience the unknown joys of the city. We must excuse her – she will in time suppress these childish expressions of sorrow and learn that women should only be noticeable when men desire to notice them."

Ming So stared at the girl and the girl stared in return at Ming So. Now, with the warmth of the rice in her stomach, she was apparently feeling far from depressed, for a smile flickered near her eyes, only to vanish again when she saw that Tung Lai Luk was watching her. Then the smile vanished, to be replaced by a look of vacancy which was her only alternative to the hatred which she really felt. But Ming So did not know this : he only saw her smile and then look vacant, so that he sniffed and turned up his nose while with facile chopsticks he rescued such dainties as his uncle had not already taken.

" The day promises to be fine," said the boy. " I

hope that the rains are really over now, for I much
doubt if this awning would keep out very much of the
water. What do you think yourself, uncle ? "

" I think as you appear to do," replied the other.
" Yes, a boat such as this is a sore trial when the
rain pours down through the awning, and everything is wet."

" Is there no space below this deck, uncle ? "

" No. In any case, the small space below is full
of merchandise. You do not imagine that I could
afford to engage a boat like this just to transport
myself – and you ? Oh, no ; before we arrived at
Ch'ang Sui the boat had been filled with the pro-
ducts of the country. The profit on sales may possibly
recoup me for some small part of the expense."

Ming So did not reply to this. He was reflecting
that his uncle was not, in the world's sense, generous.
And, that being so, he was the more puzzled to
explain such of last night's half-heard conversation
as he could now recollect. If Uncle Tung was not
generous, why had he purchased this girl from her
destitute parents for so very large a sum of money ?
Uncle Tung must have a very large staff of servants
at his house in the city, if he could thus add one to
their number at a moment's notice. . . .

Later, as the boy sat again in the bows watching
the water in front of the boat, he heard the girl
come and sit down beside him. He continued gazing
in front of him, waiting for her to speak, as he knew
all women did if you left them to themselves, and

after a little while she did begin, in a soft, wavering voice which was new to him.

> " *Jade rivers in Sz'chuen fall*
> *Down hills the hue of spring :*
> *At dawn and sunset Huang's tears*
> *Fell too, remembering.*"

Her voice ceased, and, when he looked round at her, she had dropped her eyes again to the turbid waters of the river.

" But that is great poetry," said the boy. " Such poetry as Pai Kwat, our honourable teacher, used to recite to us in the hours of school." There was no reply, so he went on : " And it is suitable poetry, too, for we move on a river flowing between banks of brilliant green, and yet, this morning, you wept. How is it that you know by heart poetry to suit your momentary mood ? "

" I know much of the work of our great poets," answered the girl's soft voice. " My mother, who came of a noble family, has often recited old poetry to me, and I have not forgotten it. Do you, then, like poetry ? "

" Of course I like poetry. Are there any who do not, except those the doors of whose hearts are closed to beauty ? " He was a little proud of that sentence. " Of all the classes of men in the State, the poet is most highly honoured. But I am surprised at your knowledge of poetry, for I seem to remember a conversation in the night, when everyone thought that I slept, with regard to the price of a girl who, my uncle said, was ill-favoured. I did not, therefore, expect to find her equipped better for revelry in a prince's court, for the wearing of the *rainbow skirt and feather jacket*, than for the exercise of the more domestic virtues." Everyone should recognise that quotation. It came from the same poem – Po Chu-I's "Everlasting Wrong." And, sure enough, at the words she smiled as she looked at him.

" So you, too, know the ' Everlasting Wrong,' do you ? In my house only my mother and I ever talked of these things : my father considered it more praiseworthy to speak of the badness of the crops, and my two brothers also spoke only of the things concerning the farm. So my father . . ."

" I see," said the boy. " It is sad to find a family in which poetry is unappreciated. For, indeed, if we do not admire the excellences of our ancestors, how shall we perfect ourselves ? " He was, quite consciously, quoting his teacher, Pai Kwat, word for word. But she need not know this. " What is your name ? "

" The only name my parents gave me is Yang Fei."

" But," the boy cried, " Yang Kuei-fei was the name of the princess whom the Emperor Huang mourned in the very poem which you have just been reciting – the ' Everlasting Wrong.' That is a peculiar thing to happen to you. I think I ought to call you Kuei-fei."

" You seem," said the girl, " both to know and to understand more than a boy of your age might be expected to know and understand. How comes it that you know not only the words of the poems which have been written, but also the stories which made the poetry ? "

" My teacher, the honourable Pai Kwat, is a great man. Not only was he skilled in literature, but they said, also, that he held communion with the spirits and could transport himself from place to place on a moonbeam. I have learned a little from him."

" As to travelling on a moonbeam I dare not venture an opinion, for a moonbeam is a very insecure sort of a vehicle. But as to your teacher's ability with brush and bamboo tablet, I judge from your own words. I judge from your words that he was a man who stood out above his lesser fellows." Her conversation was becoming animated, now that she had overcome her first shyness. " And are you, too, going with *him* " – she nodded her head towards the stern – " to the city ? "

" That is my present intention," the boy replied. " It appears that he is in need of men of honesty and brains. So . . ."

She laughed. " *A man must despise himself before others will*," she said. " But, while doubtless sitting in an office dealing with large sums of money, I shall be engaged in the menial duties of his house, under his wife's keen eye. How, then, may we talk again of these subjects ? "

Ew

"Time and opportunity may be commanded," answered the boy sententiously. "And the study of literature, being the highest and noblest of the arts, takes precedence over other more worldly considerations. So I shall await the future with confidence. But will you have the kindness to repeat again the whole of the 'Everlasting Wrong' of Po Chu-I? How does it begin?" He began reciting with particular care.

> "*The Emperor loved love : he sought*
> *Through all his wide domain*
> *For one whose lightest glance could wreck*
> *An empire – but in vain.*

Who was the woman of whom it used to be said that her glance could wreck an empire?"

The girl busied herself picking to pieces a fragment of rope which lay on the deck. "That was Madame Li, the concubine of the Emperor Han Wu-ti. She said, one day, 'One of my glances would subvert a city, two an empire.' So the Emperor sent her away from his side. It is not wise to boast." She continued, in her soft voice :

> "*Yang Kuei-fei, secluded,*
> *Her childhood's days had spent :*
> *A woman now, she nothing knows*
> *Of Love's embarrassment. . . .*"

When she had finished, the boy said : "You say poetry beautifully, much better than Pai Kwat, my teacher. Oh, but look, Kuei-fei, what fish your bait has caught."

For the crew of four, excepting the steersman, had congregated behind them. In China, poetry is recognised as the highest of the accomplishments, and it is only necessary to begin to recite the " Everlasting Wrong " or the " Ballad of Mulan " to gather a crowd at any street corner.

" Go away ! " cried Ming So. " The entertainment is over."

" Can she say the ' Ballad of Mulan ' ? " demanded the nearest man.

" Certainly she can, O seeker-after-something-fornothing, but she will not. Is this a place of public entertainment ? Go, I tell you ! " His uncle had chartered the boat, and therefore his nephew, Ming So, was a person of some small importance for the moment. The crowd of four dispersed. " They are unpleasant, common men," said Ming So.

" I do not think that a man who loves poetry can with justice be called common," she returned. " But so many men listening makes me shy. I would not have continued if I had known that they were listening to me."

" We must certainly speak more of poetry, Yang Kuei-fei."

" That is not my name. But what is yours ? "

" I am Ming So, the son of Ming Cheung Wai, who *travelled to the West* before I remember. My mother lives alone in Ha Foo with the girl Pai Mei, to whom, when I am older and have made much money, I shall offer the shelter of my roof."

" It is time enough to think of marriage when the hair has grown," the girl replied. " Now you speak of a thing of which you are ignorant. I am old enough, I, to get married. You are still an unfledged boy."

" That is as it may be," he said. " But I know that my uncle has signed a marriage-deed for me, so what you have said is just dog's wind."

The girl tossed her head and got up. " Very well – it is dog's wind, if you say that it is dog's wind. But I shall spend several happy moments, now, thinking of what you do not know about marriage ! " She left him wondering what she meant.

CHAPTER IX

OARS IN THE TWILIGHT

ONE night remained. Towards noon on the next day it was hoped that boat, cargo, and passengers would safely reach the city of Kwei Sek at the mouth of the river. Already the crew could be heard debating in increasingly strident tones the various opportunities for enjoyment or duty which stood outside the door of the coming day. Ming So was full of excitement. Only the girl Yang Fei sat silent on the mat in the stern of the boat, taking no part in these rejoicings.

Then, as they crept towards the night's rest at another, the last little village, a strange craft put off from a creek some two *li* above their evening destination. The sun had sunk half an hour ago, and twilight made the pale shadows of reeds into lances, the cry of an owl into the shriek of a lost soul. The strange boat, propelled on the now broader surface of the river by eight oars, had twice the speed of the cargo-boat, so that it was but a few minutes before she was alongside. The crews ceased rowing, and three men, attended by a fourth carrying a lantern, stepped on board. Their leader, his size exaggerated by the gleams of the lamp in the fast-departing twilight, came towards the stern with another man.

" Who is master here ? " he demanded of Uncle Tung Lai Luk. " Is this your boat ? "

" I am but a humble passenger of this boat, which belongs to a rich man who is to join us, I was told, at the village which we had hoped to reach to-night, but for this doubtless unavoidable delay," Tung replied modestly. " To what fortunate circumstance do we owe the pleasure of your visit ? " And, saying this, he must have completely frustrated his intention of appearing a man of small account, for the accent in which he spoke and a faint suspicion of irritation in his voice seemingly told the stranger precisely those things which Uncle Tung Lai Luk had not desired the stranger to know.

" Truth is not a characteristic of merchants," said the newcomer with a laugh. " This is clearly your boat. And, were it not for the inconvenience of being compelled to dispose of the cargo, we should take away your boat also. As it is, we shall take only you. Your family will be told, by those whom we leave here, that ten thousand dollars – a mere flea-bite to a man who is the possessor of so cultured a voice – will procure your freedom, and that it will be wise if your family brings here this money at sunset, after one moon has passed from to-day, since, if they omit this simple precaution, certain grosser and perhaps more decorative portions of your anatomy will be sacrificed to the God of Wealth before we let you go. I trust that you are married ? For a wife is so sweetly appreciative of the personal appearance and abilities of her husband."

" This is an outrage ! " began the merchant, but

*" Truth is not
a characteristic
of
merchants. . ."*

the other cut him short with a curt word of command. Tung Lai Luk was dragged to his feet. To Ming So his uncle's face seemed the colour of antique paper as he stood there, but only the light of the lantern lit his uncle's face, and Ming was too surprised to feel either fear or anger. His brain dully told him that these must be the river pirates of whose existence rumours had occasionally reached Ha Foo from travellers, but his attention was engaged also by the fact that in his lap, as he sat there on the deck, fell something small and hard – a cylinder some three inches long. As his uncle followed without further useless protest over the side of the boat, Ming realised that the object which he held in his hand was his uncle's *chop* – the seal which stamps the owner's name at the bottom of a document, and which is as recognisable to those who deal with him as is a European signature. Tung Lai Luk had contrived to supply his nephew not only with proof of his identity, so that he might if necessary arrange for the ransom, but also with authority to act for his uncle, who must therefore trust him somewhat more than he trusted some at least of his present captors. . . .

The sound of the raiders' oars died away; the boat, without any further orders, again took up her course for the night's anchorage, and a high patter of comment came from the crew. Yang Fei had said nothing, so the boy spoke to her.

" I was not aware that the waterways of our

Republic were so inadequately guarded and policed as seems to be the case," he said. " It is terrible that a prominent citizen like my uncle should not be able to travel in safety, and that he should be called upon, quite illegally, to make a huge payment for his freedom."

Yang Fei laughed. " I do not care," she said. " To one so poor as myself or any other member of my family these robbers are harmless, since we have nothing to lose. But your uncle, and men like him, have taken our money, and so it is fitting that some of our money should be taken from him. I wish that it could be given back to us."

" But that is wrong," protested the boy. " If, as you say, my uncle and men like him have gained money at the expense of your family, that was by fair trade. This is mere robbery, and I am surprised to hear your attempt to excuse it."

" Morality is for the rich," she said, and was silent.

The boy reflected on his future course of action. He felt very much alone now, without the guiding hand and worldly advice of his mother, however cynical she might be, and without the rather tarnished ideals of his uncle. What had they meant, those men, to do with him ? " Certain grosser and more decorative portions " of uncle Tung Lai Luk – tales of cropped ears and fingers came back to the boy. That could not possibly be allowed to happen. He would have to get his aunt, the honourable Tung Nan Tsz, to collect the sum of money as soon as he reached the city of Kwei Sek. There would be no time to waste. After all, though his uncle had given him the *chop*, a boy of thirteen could hardly hope to take the initiative in collecting so huge a sum for a ransom. Then this girl, Yang Fei. He bitterly resented her attitude, with the bitterness of the lonely and helpless. Contrary to all the basic principles of justice as expounded by the wise men who had compiled the classics of China, to the views of his teacher, Pai Kwat. . . . Little Pai Mei would never have said a thing like that. She was too sensible. Or was she ? Women were always an incalculable quantity, he reflected.

This conclusion was confirmed when, tied up at the anchorage for the last night's halt, the boat swung gently on the water and Ming returned to the bamboo shelter where the evening meal awaited him in the dim light of the swinging lantern. For the girl Yang Fei now waited on him with an attention which was capable of only one explanation – an explanation which was at once flattering and perturbing. And Ming, as he went to sleep that evening lying in his blanket at her side in the shelter, mused further on women and what they meant to him. He found the subject disquieting, the more so since Yang Fei, at her side of the shelter, was clearly not asleep, for every now and then he could hear a little smothered laugh, as if she had thought of something very funny indeed.

But youth takes no long heed of disquiet when there is no light anywhere, and soon he was dreaming happily of his sweetheart Pai Mei standing at his side, knee-deep in the pool below the waterfall in the forest at Ha Foo, and in his dream the slanting moonlight fell clear of the high trees and touched her olive skin to the semblance of a velvet intimacy. . . .

Chapter X

"THE HAPPY HEART"

Just after noon of the next day the boat was tied up to the great stone wharf in the city of Kwei Sek. The usual crowd of ricksha coolies and labourers rapidly assembled, sensing work to be had for the asking. But Ming So, very much on his dignity, instructed the master of the boat to remain at the wharf until further orders.

" You will keep this ill-mannered mob from trespassing on the boat which my unfortunate uncle has hired," he said. " As soon as I have consulted with the family, further orders will be sent to you. Until that time, do nothing. That should not be a difficult task for you." And with this parting shaft he stepped ashore, carrying in the black, shiny box all his belongings. He bore the box himself, for he dared not risk a refusal to obey orders on the part of any of the crew, and, in any case, the box was light. He hailed two rickshas.

" You will ride after me," he told Yang Fei, and sat down.

" Where to ? " enquired the runner, and for a moment Ming So's heart fell. Then he took the risk.

" Where to ? O unobservant ! Why to the house of Tung Lai Luk, and be quick about it."

The rickshas moved off, and the boy concluded with a sigh of relief that apparently his uncle was well enough known locally to make the mention of his address unnecessary. Still, he wished that he had possessed the forethought to enquire before landing. Uncle Tung Lai Luk's remaining luggage – he had only taken a single suitcase with him into his unfortunate and enforced exile – was in the second ricksha with Yang Fei. The boy leaned back in his seat and contemplated the city as if he, like his uncle, owned some considerable part of it. But his dignity was troubled by certain guffaws which the two ricksha coolies exchanged, crying to each other as they pad-padded along the road : " Tung Lai Luk ! Hai-ya ! The little ones go to Tung Lai Luk's house. Ha-ha ! " And Ming So could not quite understand the reason for this amusement.

. . . .

The two rickshas drew up before a four-storey house in one of the narrower streets, and the boy, with just enough delay to make sure that the cause of the halt was their arrival at their destination, and no other, stepped out. It would never have done to step out of the ricksha if the runners had stopped for a traffic regulation, or from shortness of breath. It would look foolish to do so, after trading on their knowledge of the whereabouts of his uncle's house. . . .

The house was large in comparison with the others

in the street, but he noticed that its brass scroll-work entrance was copied, farther down the street, by several other apparently similar establishments. He began to be consumed by a curiosity as to the precise nature of his uncle's trade.

In answer to his call, a small serving-maid appeared at the door. Behind her a porter lounged in a wicker chair.

"I wish to see the honourable wife of Tung Lai Luk," said Ming So, and the child smiled.

"Many have wished that," she returned, "but seldom without advancing a reason."

"I am Tung's nephew," he told her. "Now, lead on."

She shrugged her shoulders, but led on. There were three flights of stairs and one corridor to traverse before a door opened and he entered the room beyond with Yang Fei.

"This boy says that he is your nephew," the small maid said. "Shall I show him out again, and tell the porter to add to his speed?"

"But why . . . ? Where is the honourable Tung?"

The woman sitting at the far side of the room rose and came towards him. Ming was surprised to see a much younger woman than he had expected. Of middle height, as a Chinese girl should be, she had the high cheek-bones of the Northern Manchu, while her movements, sudden and graceful, betokened Southern blood as well. How had his far-from-young uncle managed to marry this radiant being? The boy noted the touch of rice-powder which accentuated the redness of her lips, the perfect blackness of her " moth's eyebrows," the lazy yet fiery glow of her dark eyes. She raised her arm with a flash of embroideries in the light from the windows in the roof. " Where is he? " she demanded, her forefinger threatening him.

Ming So recoiled a step before her. Then he took from an inner pocket the *chop* which his uncle had dropped in his lap as the pirates had led him away. He removed the small cap, pushed up the red ink-pad inside the tube with his finger, and then, pressing the *chop* itself on to the pad, withdrew it and made, on the palm of his small hand, the impression which the *chop* bore. " Tung," she read, as the boy held up his palm for her to see. " That is the *chop* of the honourable Tung, my husband. Where is he, and how did you come to have possession of that *chop* ? "

" May I sit down ? " Ming So asked. " I thank you. Events over which neither I nor my unhappy uncle had any control have led, I greatly fear, to a long and possibly expensive separation of husband and wife. Last night, just before we reached our evening anchorage . . ."

When he had finished, he laid the *chop* on the table. " It is for you to say what should be done," he told her. " For my part, I do not like the threat of the man to remove certain ornamental portions of my uncle. I think that the man meant this threat seriously, and I advise payment, to avoid the greater evil which would otherwise befall him."

" Ten thousand dollars ! " the woman shrieked. " And how, O fool, do you imagine that I can find ten thousand dollars, and how do you think that we are going to continue to live here if we pay ten thousand dollars ? It is all your fault. You should have warned the crew when you saw the other boat approaching, so that flight might have saved you from them."

" They had eight oars : we had three," Ming So replied simply. " You may be sure that, if it had been possible, we should have escaped. But it was not possible."

And now, as women will in such circumstances, Tung's wife wept, and Ming So watched her weep. When the sound had subsided somewhat, he spoke softly.

" If you are willing, my aunt, I will go and inter-view my uncle's friends, so that they may advance the money which you find it impossible to collect. For indeed it would be undutiful of us to let him suffer a fate so disfiguring and so unpleasant to both of you. Then, further, there is the case of this girl, whose name appears to be Yang Fei. Or so she told me. My uncle purchased her from her impoverished family on the way down the river. Would it not be possible to sell her again, if you could find a buyer, and to devote the proceeds to my uncle's ransom ? "

" That ! " shrieked Tung's wife suddenly, out of

her sobs. " That ! Why, she is worth but the smallest fraction of the immense sum which, you tell me, we must raise. She will earn her price in a week. What did you say that the honourable Tung Lai Luk paid for her ? "

" I do not know. My uncle began by offering a hundred and fifty dollars, but then I went to sleep and I do not know at what figure the sale was concluded."

" You slept ! Of course you slept ! More than a hundred and fifty dollars ? Waste ! Now go from my presence. I must think, and when I have thought I will send for you to tell you my decision." She issued rapid instructions to the small serving-maid. " Go now. Leave me."

Yang Fei came last, as usual.

.　　.　　.　　.　　.　　.　　.　　.

Ming So found himself in a small room on the top floor. The room was so small, in fact, that he was reminded of the rattan shelter on the boat. Strangely enough, Yang Fei had apparently been allotted a similar room, next door, which was a strange thing to contemplate where a servant was concerned, the boy reflected. Still, if even their servants had separate rooms, the Tung establishment must be rich enough to produce the ten thousand dollars for the ransom without much difficulty. . . . He disposed his property around him and changed his coat. Then, while he was hesitating what to do next, there came a rap at the door with the finger-nails, and Yang Fei entered.

"Ah Ming!" she cried, and her agitation was such that he hardly realised that her manner of address was regrettably familiar. "I have just discovered what nature of house this is! I was standing at my door when another girl came, followed by an old woman in black and a young man. They all three went into the room next to mine, and after a while the old woman came out again, carrying money, which she counted. She fluttered the bank-notes between her fingers and then went away. I listened, then, at the door of the room where the girl and the young man had gone in and . . ." Her eyes filled with tears. "Alas, I do not know what will become of me!"

"Shut the door first," said the boy. "This affects you, not me, but I do not see why you should allow a draught to enter as well as yourself. Indeed, this is a strange story which you tell me. So that is the nature of my uncle's business, is it? Well, there are worse, and the business will not be subject to trade depression, I imagine. But it certainly is surprising. And you are crying now. Why?"

"I do not want to stay here," wailed the girl. "I want to go back to my village, now, and starve."

"But starvation is painful," he said. "No – that would be foolish. In any case, you are hardly likely to find that much work is expected of you so soon after your arrival here. Though I must confess that
Fw

I thought, when my uncle purchased you, that you were to be just a serving-maid, like the child who let us in."

" Listen ! " she whispered. From the next room but one came laughter, then a girl's voice singing. " She is happy ! " Suddenly the voice stopped. " Ah ! He no longer desires her to play to him. Ah Ming, this thing is bad."

The boy had got up.

" I am going to see the things which happen in this house. I shall go downstairs and find out. You may remain here, if you wish to dry your tears in my room rather than in your own. And have you reflected that you are lucky to have a room of your own ? It is not usual, in the case of purchased girls, of *mui-tsai*. . . ." He went out.

The stairways were wide and hung with curtains, but Ming met nobody until he reached the street level. Here was the entrance-hall again, and he noticed what he had not seen before – that the brass-work could be slid across, if required, like a barrier, by the porter who sat, or rather lay, in the bamboo chair at the side of it. This porter winked at Ming So.

" Well, little one, and what are you doing here ? You are surely too young to justify me in asking you which girl of our collection you are desirous of enjoying ? "

" I am the nephew of the honourable Tung Lai Luk," said Ming So, and the porter laughed.

" Therefore I have come to see what happens in this remarkable house. Tell me, where does a man eat his rice, for I am hungry ? "

The porter laughed again.

" I have heard many times that tale of a nephew," he said. " It is a very old tale, old as the mountains of Shansi. No, it appears that, in spite of your age, you may be here for the same purpose as many another who values the moment above the morning after. Which girl do you want ? There are many here, all different and all alike."

" I desire no girl. I desire to eat rice," protested the boy. " My uncle would not be pleased if he knew that I was hungry and that his porter lay on his back in a chair, unwilling to help. My room is on the top floor, and its number is eighty-seven. Unless rice is brought rapidly, there will be unpleasantness." He turned on his heel. Then, as an afterthought, he added : " I shall require at least two bowls of rice."

As he ascended the stairs again he encountered a young man whose breath smelled of wine.

" Yes, run upstairs if you like, little one," this man cried after him. " You will not always be able to run so fast." And, indeed, the man who had thus addressed Ming appeared to find some difficulty in getting downstairs himself, for he was holding on to the rail which ran down the opposite side of the stairs from the wall. Ming took no notice and went on. At the top of the house he paused, for there were voices in his own bedroom. Then he went on again and entered, to find Yang Fei standing and talking to another girl, whose extremely bright pyjamas caught the boy's eye at once.

" This is Tung's nephew," said Yang Fei.

" And I," said the other girl, " am called Lien Fa – The Lily. I hear that your uncle has been captured by pirates, and that his wife hopes to be able to pay ten thousand dollars for his release. I should have thought her well quit of him. If I had men like that coming to see me, I should give up business. He is fat and slow and stupid."

" It would not be right to let him suffer the forcible removal of ears," replied Ming So. " I cannot agree that it would be right. After all . . ."

" You will talk less of right when you have been here a little while longer," said The Lily. " In Tung's establishment – which calls itself, as you will have doubtless seen, ' The Happy Heart ' – there is no room for justice. All the bedrooms are full already. There are very few rooms that are not bedrooms."

A knock sounded on the door, and the little serving-maid appeared.

" If this woman Yang will follow me, I will show her where she may obtain rice and rice-bowls for you both," said the child. " Do you want yours, Lien Fa ? The girl Yang might bring it."

" Yes ; take her," replied The Lily. When the door had closed again she continued in an amused voice : " That is the only advantage of 'The Happy Heart' – the meals are at no fixed hours. They cannot be, owing to the nature of the business. One may eat rice whenever hunger comes – and hunger comes at strange times to us girls. You are lucky – you can have yours brought to you. But I did not know that Tung had a nephew. His family must have been less fat and useless than he is. Tell me about yourself." She sat down on the boy's bed. " Do you not wonder at the possession of a bed like this, a big bed, instead of being compelled to sleep on the floor ? Yes, that is another advantage of 'The Happy Heart.' Now, tell me – where did you live before you came here ? "

Ming So began to lose a little of his shyness as he sat there on his own bed with this strange girl beside him. He told her about his home in Ha Foo, and had got as far as a disquisition on the virtues of little Pai Mei when the girl Yang Fei returned with three bowls of rice and one of savoury meat and vegetables, in a lacquer carrier. With her arrival, Ming's flow of words deserted him.

" I will tell you more of these matters another day," he said. " For the moment I am hungry, and I suggest that we should eat."

Lien Fa laughed and held out her hand for the bowl of rice.

Chapter XI

THE BEARER OF A NOBLE NAME

EXCEPT that his sleep had been somewhat disturbed by sounds of laughter, music, and similar noises from adjacent rooms, Ming So had passed a comfortable night. In the light of the dawn he looked round him at the little room, taking stock. But no sooner had he begun to reflect on " The Happy Heart " and its occupants than instantly he remembered the predicament of his uncle, and the necessity for action on the part of that deplorable woman, his aunt. She had promised to send for him yesterday to discuss what might be done about the ransom, and here was the next morning.

He sprang to his feet and put on his outer clothing. Outside the door, in the passage, the small servant-girl was sweeping up an assortment of empty cigarette packets and the husks of melon-seeds.

" Where is your mistress ? " the boy demanded. " I must speak with her at once. It is most important that I should speak with her."

" The noble lady," said the child, using a very respectful title, " does not rise until towards the middle of the hour of the Horse, when the sun stands highest in the heavens."

" But she will rise earlier this morning – I know she will," the boy persisted.

" She has not risen, for I came from her room a moment past, and she was still sleeping. To rouse her would lead to much unpleasantness, for she possesses no light hand."

In the face of this, Ming started off back to his bedroom. Life was going to be extraordinarily dull, with nowhere but his bedroom to go to. . . . Yang Fei came round the corner of the passage.

" Come," she said. " Lien Fa is awake, and wants to see you. I think that you amuse her."

" I have nothing better to do," replied Ming So, " and therefore I shall come with you. But otherwise she should have asked me in vain. Amuse her, indeed ! It is she who amuses me."

Lien Fa was still in bed, her great black eyes regarding him over the bed-coverings with evident pleasure.

" Here is our little talking-bird," she cried. " Come in, and tell me a tale of your village of Ha Foo. No ! You must not sit there – move the music-box, Yang Fei. How should I entertain my visitors if you sat on my music-box ? " And, when the younger girl had moved the gramophone to the floor, Lien Fa sat up in bed. " Come, sit here and talk to me. I like to hear you speak – it reminds me of the time when I had two little brothers of my own, like you."

" Are they dead, then ? " asked Ming So, pre-pared to condole with her.

" No – I have left my family, so that I can no

longer call them my brothers. Besides, they have married and gone to other cities. They are very respectable citizens. Open the window a little, Yang Fei – there were many evil-smelling cigarettes smoked here last night, and I have a small headache. Now, little one, talk."

" I cannot talk freely when so important a matter as my uncle's ransom goes unattended to," replied the boy. " I am sad to think that his wife is so undutiful as to sleep, to be sleeping now, when she ought to be up and out, collecting money for my uncle's ransom."

" Is it really as innocent as it appears ? " demanded Lien Fa of the ceiling. " Is it possible that such an unsoiled mind really exists ? Tell me, little one, what did you dream of ? "

" I dreamed of Pai Mei, whom I am to marry," he answered. " Again I was walking with her up the path to the temple where we parted – again I was leading her, that night my uncle came to Ha Foo, along the forest path to the pool where, under the waterfall, we bathed in the moonlight."

" Tell me," said Lien Fa suddenly, " is this Pai Mei of yours beautiful ? "

" I think her so," he replied. " To me she represents woman, and I measure others by her. How far short they fall ! "

The girl lazily got out of bed. Yang Fei sat on the floor, watching her open-mouthed as she poured water into the hand-basin and then took off the jacket of her pyjamas, for Yang Fei was not accustomed to washing when you were obviously not dirty.

" I am called The Lily," said Lien Fa, smiling back at Ming So over her olive shoulder as she washed. Here was none of the undeveloped child – the muscles rippled gently up and down her arm as she rubbed a wet cloth over her neck. " I am called The Lily, and you measure me by your Pai Mei ! Foolish boy ! Your Pai Mei will never be as beautiful as I. Look. Will she ? "

Somewhat embarrassed, the boy looked at her as she stood there in her brilliant pyjama trousers with the wet cloth in her hand. So that was how girls developed when they grew up, he thought.

" Pai Mei is different," he said loyally. " I do not think that she will ever look as you look now, but I do not really wish her to resemble you. She is different."

" Little fool ! " said The Lily, and returned to her washing, mildly amused. " You know so much of women, you do. Of Yang Fei here, for instance. A pretty pair you would make. Yang, turn the handle of the music-box as I showed you yesterday."

Yang Fei put on a record, inserted a needle, and wound up the gramophone. Lien Fa completed her washing to the accompaniment of a Chinese song which told of girls gathering reeds in the river when a prince passed by.

" I wish a few princes would come here," said she petulantly. " I have also some foreign records. Would you like to hear them ? "

" I think if you do not mind, that I will return to my own room. I have just remembered that I have to write a letter to my honourable mother, and another letter as well."

" To little Pai Mei, to tell her that you have seen me washing ? " laughed The Lily.

" I do not think that I shall mention your washing," said Ming So seriously. " It would not interest her." And he went out to write his letters.

Lien Fa remained pensive for a moment. Then, with a sudden access of energy, she flung the wet cloth at the retreating boy and kicked off her trousers. " Little fool ! " she cried again, and Yang Fei put on the other side of the record.

.   .   .   .

At noon he was fetched to go to the wife of Tung Lai Luk. In her top-lit room she sat, where he had seen her last, beside a huge blackwood screen decorated with gold dragons.

" I have been thinking about you and what we shall do with you," she began. " Have you any idea what my unfortunate husband intended ? "

" I fancy," said the boy, " that he intended to let me help him in the business which I understood he did here in Kwei Sek. But, now that I have seen the nature of this business, I am not so sure, for what could I do to help him in a house such as this, full of girls ? I cannot keep girls in order for him."

" No, that is true. Sit down, child. I think that what your uncle wished was for you to live here and keep him better informed than he used to be as to what goes on – the intrigues which there are bound to be in a house full of girls."

Ming So seated himself on the edge of a porcelain stool. " While I am, of course, anxious to do whatever my uncle intended, that might of necessity be altered by the changed circumstances. He has been taken by brigands who threaten to remove portions of him, and I should like to know what you are going to do in the matter of his ransom. That seems to me a more pressing matter, and I should like to know . . ."

" If you would think less and talk less, you might be of more use to everybody," she interrupted him. " Do you think that I am not doing everything which I can do ? Do you think that I am leaving it to chance ? Last night, after seeing you in the afternoon, I began at once to approach people who may be able to help. You can set your foolish little mind at rest about the steps which we shall take for your uncle's release. Now, until I give you further orders, you will move about amongst the girls and report to me every day at noon all the gossip which you hear. You should not find this difficult, since you have, I presume, struck up an acquaintance with the ugly little girl whom my unfortunate husband so unwisely bought. What friends has she made ? "

" She was playing the music-box of the girl called Lien Fa, The Lily," answered the boy. " That is all I know."

" Good. Then from her you will hear all that matters, for Lien Fa has a tongue which never ceases wagging save when she sleeps, and that is not often. Now go."

Ming So decided that he did not particularly like this woman, his aunt. He saw also that she was clever, for she had turned the conversation from the ransom to gossip amongst the girls. How if she did not really want her husband back ? Lien Fa had as much as hinted at this.

" Who saw the noble lady yesterday afternoon ? " he demanded suddenly of the little serving-girl.

" Yesterday afternoon ? There was a seller of silk, and three women, and then a man from the Government – he stopped a long while. That was all, I think. Why do you desire to learn this ? "

" And do you desire to learn why I desire to learn ? Women were ever curious ! " He went into his bedroom and shut the door behind him. Time looked like hanging heavily on his hands. He would go out and post the two letters which had written. But as he felt through his pockets, where he was sure he had put the letters, his hand encountered another piece of paper. He drew it out and read :

" If you would ask your mother's advice, call instead on the very honourable descendant of the Master, one Kung Hiao Ling, who lives at the corner of Market Street and Frog's Lane, in the city of Kwei Sek. His advice would be mine, for he has all the wisdom of his ancestor, Confucius, and I knew him when I was young. Remind him, if he will condescend to see you, of the girl who gave him his hat when he dropped it at the Eastern Gate."

He recognised his mother's writing. But how ? He did not remember hearing his mother say anything about this paper. . . . She must have put it in the pocket when she packed his clothes. He almost ran down the stairs.

" Going out ? " said the porter lazily.

" Or coming in backwards," answered the boy. " I go to the post office. Tell me its whereabouts."

" You follow this street until you come to the wine-shop. There you turn to the left : that is Market Street. As far along that road as a man may see in a light mist lies the post office."

" Your courtesy is more marked than I had hoped," returned the boy.

Without much difficulty he found the post office and despatched his letters. Then he searched for Frog's Lane, and finally located the house where

Kung lived – the very wine-shop which the porter had mentioned. The boy ascended two flights of stairs, guided by information from the folk on each floor, and finally found himself in a single great room, running the full depth of the building, on the highest floor. A man sat cross-legged on a mat in the very centre of the room. A few screens indicated that more domestic details might be found behind them, by those who cared to look.

" Have I the incredible honour of addressing Kung Hiao Ling ? " he asked, abashed in the presence of a man who watched him from below heavy lids as he sat there immobile on his mat. " I fear that I interrupt your studies ? "

The man inclined his head.

" I am the unworthy bearer of a noble name, and you do not interrupt my studies," he said. " Go on. . . ."

" Once, at the Eastern Gate, a girl picked up and gave back to you the hat which you had dropped there," said Ming So.

" That happened to me – long ago. What of it ? "

" The girl was my mother."

Kung rose to his feet and bowed. " Welcome," he said. " So polite a mother had a son ? It is almost incredible. But . . ." He held out his hand for the paper – scanned it. " Your mother rates me too highly. But tell me your trouble, and I will give you advice, if I have any to give."

" I am the son of Ming Nai," began the boy, in the time-honoured formula which begins all stories.

" Sit down with me and continue," interposed Kung Hiao Ling. " Now, go on."

.   .   .   .

" You have, of course, written to your mother to inform her of these facts ? " Kung asked.

" I have written. But, as I wrote the letter before the interview with the wife of my uncle, I was not able to tell my mother how, in my opinion, insufficient effort was being made to collect the ransom. But then there was the officer of the Government who called on my aunt yesterday afternoon and stayed for a long time. It is possible that he came on my aunt's invitation, and that she seeks, by means of military force, to free my uncle without a cash payment. Is that possible ? "

" It is possible," agreed the other, " though it is hardly likely. For the officials of this new Government look askance on establishments such as that of your uncle. In fact these establishments have, in some provinces, been closed by order of the local Government. Here we are too reactionary at present, perhaps, for so drastic an action on their part, but it will come. What I intended to convey to you was that even here the officials look on the business of your uncle with disapproval, and would therefore be unlikely to make efforts to release him."

" But," the boy cried, " I feel that it is my duty to set him free. After all, it was on my account that he undertook the journey, and therefore it was because of me that he was captured."

" You unduly flatter your importance, I think," Kung Hiao Ling smiled. " I do not think that a man like Tung Lai Luk, whom I have met and (I am afraid) disliked, would journey so far up the river just to see to the future of a small nephew. No : the girl whom he purchased, and the fact that the boat was full of merchandise, both show that the affair of bringing you down to the city of Kwei Sek was only incidental to his other interests. Besides, he hoped, if what your aunt says is true, to make use of you as a collector of gossip. But one can never trust women, as you will discover."

" That is very true," agreed the boy.

" Well, let the matter stop there for the moment. I will enquire from certain friends of mine whether she has approached the Government about releasing your uncle. I will also, through other friends, find out whether she has attempted to borrow the money for his ransom. You will doubtless be able to find cause to go again to the post office to-morrow, when you have written to your mother your account of to-day's events. Come, then, to see me at the same time, and I may be fortunate enough to have news for you. But do not talk, nor tell to your excellent aunt too much of what you hear from the girls. A still tongue is worth uncounted gold."

"I will do as you say," the boy promised.

"And, on your way downstairs, tell the master of the wine-shop that my wine-jar is empty. Walk well."

"Walk well," echoed Ming So, in parting politeness.

.   .   .   .

In an upper room of the establishment known as "The Happy Heart" two were talking in the dark. Their voices, at any rate, were very close to each other.

"She is unaccountably reluctant to arrange for your freedom," said the man's voice. "I cannot understand her reluctance. Have I not given her, or at any rate offered, everything that a woman in her position could desire? Have I not even given her what I would have preferred to have given only to you?"

"You have," the girl agreed. "She is a water-rat, and the daughter of a water-rat, and I hate her." She paused. "But, then, you have given her this thing of which you speak, only once, or twice, or ten times. She desires it not once, or twice, or ten times, but always. Do you not realise that, O blind lover?"

There was only a rustling now. Then the man's voice replied. "I see that, but I do not desire her. I desire you, sweetheart, and to give to the water-rat what I desire to give to you only, fills my heart

Gw

with loathing and my mouth with a bitter taste."

" Is it not therefore possible, O my lover, that she understands your feeling – the feeling of which you have just spoken ? May she not know how insincere is your gift ? Perhaps that may explain why she still withholds her willingness, why she puts needless obstacles and difficulties in our way. But " – and the girl's voice became tender – " am I worthy, then, of all this trouble ? Do you so much desire me ? "

" The land desires the rain, and the rain desires the land," he answered. " Have I then spoken what you would have had me speak ? But do you think that my father could help me ? He is, as you are aware, unscrupulous and without heart, but for me, his son . . ."

" Your father can do little if she does not wish it," said the girl. " She is as a granite rock which the water wears away in a year less than a man can measure. Her heart is of flint. It may be broken, but never touched."

" What you say is true," replied the man. " In fact, her demands have lately become greater. I have spoken to my father on the subject, but he only laughed, saying that women never know what they want."

There was silence for a space now in this upper room in " The Happy Heart," where these two debated their future. There seemed little more that might usefully be said. But, after a while, the girl's voice continued : " I think that she desires you, and in that case I cannot imagine why, as all the house knows, she has at the present moment not you, but your father, in her room. I cannot but feel that here is matter which calls for explanation."

" Do not talk so much," the man's voice replied, laughing. " All will solve itself, and for the moment we are very happy, are we not ? "

" Yes, but . . ." began the girl, when her voice was lost in laughter.

Chapter XII

TRAGI-COMEDY

THE day had passed in unendurable peace. To Ming So's enquiries they replied that Tung's wife was busy and could talk with no one. Lien Fa was asleep, and, when he wakened her, swore at him and went to sleep again. Yang Fei proved unbearably dull – he began to realise that in reciting the " Ballad of Everlasting Wrong " she had exhausted her repertoire, or so it seemed. The porter, whom the boy approached in desperation, was reading a novel, and resented interruption.

So the afternooon and evening passed in utter boredom. Ming So began to wonder how he could possibly live in " The Happy Heart " for very much longer. He missed the unending work and incident of the country, finding the city spiritually a Gobi desert of dullness.

It was about ten o'clock, when the life of the establishment showed signs of beginning and Ming thought of bed as a refuge from inaction, that Lien Fa brought a man friend into Ming's room. This man was not more than twenty-five, and Lien Fa's attitude towards him indicated that not only her business and professional instincts were affected here. The boy suddenly realised that The Lily, too, had a real sweetheart. Only the relations of the

two lacked the innocence of Ming's relations with
Pai Mei.

" Here is the callow cavalier," cried Lien Fa
to her man. " He knows all about girls, he says –
he, at his age. And behind that door " – she pulled
in Yang Fei by the arm – " stands another innocent.
Behold the two love-birds. And, even so, he has
another girl elsewhere."   She struck an attitude,
and the man laughed.

" Well, you stand in no danger, Lien Fa, from
the girl's competition, so far as beauty is concerned ! "
he said.   " And if this callow boy can see in her that
which makes a man forget himself, he has weaker
eyesight than I have. What was the amusement of
which you spoke, O Lily ? Does it concern these
two ? "

" It does concern them, very closely," answered
Lien Fa. " Do you stand here by the door and pre-
vent their escape. I will do the rest. Watch ! "

Ming So interrupted her. " I should be glad if
you would leave my bedroom," he said.   " Honoured as I am to meet this lover of yours, I feel that
sleep is the best occupation for the evening, and it
was my intention to go to bed."

The Lily laughed a little uncontrollably, and he
saw, to his disgust, that she had been drinking. Her
man stood in the doorway, mildly amused.

" You shall go to bed," cried The Lily ; " you
shall certainly go to bed. But for our amusement
you shall not go to bed alone. First, I will remove

from this room all clothing and bed-linen to the room of the girl Yang Fei.   Then you shall see what is to be seen."

"You are mad !" cried Ming So.   "Those clothes are mine : put them down !"

"See the lion defending its fur !" said Lien Fa, collecting clothes.   "Come on, if you are so inclined.   Try to stop me !"   She pushed the boy violently back into Yang Fei, snatched up the bedding, and carried it out of the room.   "Keep them there, Ah Loo," she cried as she went out.

Ming made a dash for the door, to be seized by the arm and held in a grip from which he could not escape.

"The boy struggles like a hare in a net," said the man, Ah Loo, holding him without effort.   "Come back and do what you propose, while I have him fast."

Ming So knew, as he struggled vainly, that the scene was photographing itself indelibly on his memory.   He saw his black case in the corner, lying open, while all his spare clothes were carried out of the room.   Yang Fei, in another corner, with utter consternation in her moon-like face, took no part in the proceedings.   The bed had been stripped down to the mattress : the curtains of the room were removed.

"Help !" cried Ming So, and the man put a hand over his mouth.

"Stop yelling," he said, "or I will twist your arm, so."

Then Lien Fa came back to the door, entered, and shut it after her. " Now," she said, and her eyes were bright with wine, " now. Let us make them blush. I like seeing children blush, when they do not know why they are blushing. It will amuse you, Ah Loo. Hold him tightly – he is very like an eel." But even the boy's wriggling availed little when Lien Fa took hold of him. . . .

Freed, the boy crouched in a corner, his outraged modesty welling up in angry tears. He sank his head on his hands, so that he did not see Lien Fa seize the girl Yang Fei in her turn. He only heard little sobs – " Don't ! It is not right ! " – and the laughter of Ah Loo as he watched.

" I will tell the officers of the Government," sobbed the boy. " They will punish you both."

Lien Fa laughed and set Yang Fei at liberty. " Poor little fool ! I always said that you were a fool. Ah Loo, or his father, constitutes a most important part of the Government. And do you think that your word will be taken against his ? Do you not know that Ah Loo had a long interview with the noble lady Tung yesterday about pur- chasing my freedom ? Silly ! "

" They make a fine pair, thus, seen crouching in corners without their clothes," chuckled the man. " Although she is an ugly little thing, and he is skinny. Still, it is amusing. What do we do next, Lien Fa, to amuse ourselves ? "

" I think that we go away," The Lily replied in a

whisper, "and leave them alone together. After a little while they will be less like wild beasts crouching there in the corners of the room. Come ; I will carry the clothes of these two, and we will lock the door on the outside. Then, by and by, we shall come back."

"He is very nearly a man, but not quite," was the last thing Ming heard Ah Loo say as he shut the bedroom door and turned the key in the lock.

.   .   .   .

When the sounds of their feet had died away, Ming So rose to his feet and blew out the lamp.

"So," he said. "I do not know what we can do now, for they are excited with wine and may not return for hours to let us out. It does not matter very much for you, Yang Fei, for you are only a girl. But for a man like me – the indignity . . ." He became incoherent for a moment as the memory flooded back to him. "I shall leave this house to-morrow. I shall leave it as soon as I can."

Yang Fei's voice sounded for the first time. "It is not warm, Ming So, and my skin is already becoming chilled. What shall we do ? "

"There you go ! " Ming groped his way to the bed and sat on the edge of the mattress. "Troubling about the coldness of your skin ! It does not matter, I tell you. The question is, how am I to escape ? That mule's daughter Lien Fa shall suffer for this. I will tell the noble lady Tung how she

has behaved. I will tell the Government. I will
tell . . ." He stopped suddenly. " The window !
Can we get out that way ? " He ran across and
threw it open. There was not here the usual ver-
andah running along the side of the house, and in
the dark, even, he could see the space of bare, blank
wall between him and the window of Yang Fei's
room, next door. Below, out of sight but not out of
hearing, the stream ran bubbling with the late
spring rains, at the base of the building. There was
no escape. He shut the window with a bang and
swore. " She is the daughter of a pole-cat. May
the gods afflict her and her unpleasing lover with
diseases such that they will be objects of disgust to
each other and everyone else. May . . ."

" What is the use ? " demanded Yang Fei as she
sat beside him on the edge of the mattress, " of
cursing them like that ? You are wasting your
breath. What must be, must be, and it seems that
we are fated to spend a few hours together. We
may as well not spend them in useless sorrow.
Lien Fa and her man will come and let us out some
time, and until then we can sleep."

" But I have no clothes to sleep in, and no bedding to sleep under," the boy complained. " They
have left us not a stitch of clothing, not a blanket
nor a rug. They shall suffer for it, I tell you ! "

" It is not as cold as I thought at first," Yang Fei
murmured in the darkness. It seemed as if her
voice were nearer, as she had shifted towards him.

" There are two of us, and two can be warmer than
one." Her arm went round his shoulders, and
though he shivered at the touch he remained still.
" Poor little Ah Ming ! Go to sleep and forget it
until they return. Come, I will tell you again the
Ballad of Everlasting Wrong :

> *The Emperor loved love : he sought*
> *Through all his wide domain*
> *For one whose lightest glance could wreck*
> *An empire . . .*

Now, go to sleep, or I will not tell you more. . . .

> *An empire, but in vain.*
>
> *Yang Kuei-fei, secluded,*
> *Her childhood's days had spent :*
> *A woman now, she nothing knew*
> *Of Love's embarrassment.*"

Her voice went on through the poem. By and
by the boy's stiff shoulders relaxed, and Yang Fei
gathered him into her arms, as the unfortunate
Emperor must have gathered his favourite, as she
continued the immortal poem of Po Chu-I.

.   .   .   .

Yang Fei sat stiffly on the mattress, holding the
sleeping boy in her arms. Her right leg had gone
to sleep, and every now and then she shivered.
Suddenly she heard the key turn again in the lock.
She must have been sleeping, or dozing. The door
opened, and Ah Loo came in.

" 'Sh ! " whispered Yang Fei. " He is sleeping. Do not wake him."

Ah Loo shut the door softly and set down the lamp which he was carrying. " I will fetch his bedding from next door," he said.

" And my clothes, please," said Yang Fei, but the man shook his head as he went out. He was wearing, she noticed, a pair of The Lily's flamboyant pyjamas. By and by he returned.

" Set him down on this blanket," said Ah Loo. " He will not wake up. So. Now we will cover him up and leave him. Lien Fa is asleep, which is surprising. Come. Softly ! "

The door shut behind them, and Ming So slumbered on comfortably in his untidy mass of blankets, like a small, hairless dormouse.

.   .   .   .

The boy woke. It was still night, though the faintest gleam showed through the window. He seemed to have heard a cry in his dream as he slept. He sat up and listened. The house was in utter silence, and, still half-asleep, he was just about to compose himself again in the warm nest of the blankets when he realised that he was naked. In a flash all the events of the earlier night returned. Where was the girl ?

" Yang Fei," he whispered, and no answer came. He slid out of bed and lit the lamp with a match from the box beside it. The room was empty but for himself. They must have gone and left him.

All his rage flowed back now. His clothes were in the next room. . . .

Ming So opened the door of Yang Fei's room, holding the lamp before him. The fickle gleam of the little oil flame shone in the corners of the room. He saw his clothes piled together where Lien Fa had dropped them. But he did not look long at his clothes, for on the bed, curiously yellow in the light of the tiny lamp, lay Ah Loo, the lover of The Lily. He was lying strangely quiet, and as the boy looked more closely he saw that the white sheet was white only where it fell to the floor in a motionless cascade. On the bed, where Ah Loo lay, the white sheet became inexplicably dark grey – dark red. He touched the sheet, and his finger stuck slightly as he withdrew it.

The boy almost screamed, but it seemed as if his voice would not work. Ah Loo had been murdered ! Ming crept from the room, automatically sucked his sticky finger, and then spat at the salt taste of blood. What should he do ? Could they all be sleeping ? Who had thus murdered Ah Loo, the lover of The Lily ?

He crept along to Lien Fa's room and opened the door with extreme care.

Yang Fei, her eyes wide with horror, sat looking mutely at him from the bed. Her black hair had become unbraided, hanging in untidy festoons round her face. Of the room's usual tenant there was no sign : the gramophone had vanished.

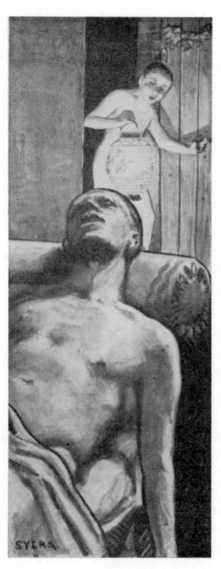

Ming So
opened
the door

" What has happened ? " Ming asked in a whisper. " There is the man, Ah Loo, lying in a pool of blood on your bed. Did you kill him ? "

The girl said nothing, still staring at him with an expression which he had never before seen on her face. She hardly appeared to see him at all : her wide-open eyes stared through him at the door. Then, at last, she spoke.

" He took me in there," she said, and Ming could hardly hear the words. " Lien was asleep, and he threatened to wake her. Also, you were asleep where I had left you when he came to open the door and let me out, and I did not want to wake you. So I went with him." She burst into a storm of silent, dry-eyed sobbing. " O-oh ! And afterwards, when I was wanting to kill myself, I must have made a noise, for Lien Fa woke and came in. She had a long knife in her hand, and I saw her strike him as he lay. The point of the knife cut me, here. . . . Then she laughed and went away. I was too frightened even to cry out. I heard Lien Fa go out of my room and then her footsteps went along the corridor."

" She ran away ? " demanded the boy.

" When she had gone, I could not bear to sit there with the dead man, so I came in here. I could not come to your room, after what had happened to me, for I was ashamed. And then you came, now. That is all I know. O-oh, what shall I do ? He loved me, like that, and now he is dead, and they will think that I killed him."

Ming So took a decision as he put on his trousers from the pile on the floor in the room with the murdered man. This matter was too big to hush up : he must tell the police. The two of them might manage to push the body over the window-sill into the stream below, but they could hardly remove all the bloody bedding. And Lien Fa had gone, and there would be sure to be questions. Anyway, why try to conceal what should be known ? He went back to Lien Fa's room.

" Come," he said, and the girl Yang Fei followed him meekly. " Put on your clothes from this pile. Then go back into my room and stay there. I am going to telephone to the police. I do not know how to use the telephone, but that will solve itself. Where is there a telephone ? "

" There is one in the room where the lady Tung sleeps," said Yang Fei. " Oh, they will think that I did it. I wish I had. I shall say that I killed him, and then they will kill me. I do not wish to live, after . . ."

" You are a foolish woman," replied the boy. " Go to my room when you have dressed – take all my other clothes and the bedclothes back with you, quickly. Action cures sorrow. I go to telephone."

He padded softly along the corridor in his bare feet. Through the skylights the dawn was brushing grey on black and pink on grey. But Ming So did not attend to these things. The room belonging to his aunt was not locked, and he found the telephone quite easily. Could he use this strange machine without waking the occupant of the room? He looked towards the bed and revised his phraseology. The occupants of the room, he amended. He could not see who the man was. Then he lifted the receiver from the hook. From a long distance, it seemed, a voice asked:

"What number?"

"Send police, now, to Tung's house," he whispered. "Tung Lai Luk. 'The Happy Heart.' There has been a killing. One man is dead – a Government official – Ah Loo, she called him. Room eighty-six. Quick! I cannot say more."

He set the receiver down on the table and went softly out of the room to comfort Yang Fei.

CHAPTER XIII

TO LIE LIKE A GENTLEMAN

PO FENG HSI, Chief of the City Police, sat at his office desk, tapping gently on the blotting-pad with a pencil. Opposite to him, on an uncomfortable, hard chair, sat the wife of Tung Lai Luk. The fact that the Chief's eye twinkled, while the not ungenerous lines of his build recalled the Chinese proverb that a fat man is a happy man, availed nothing to comfort Tung's wife, for she realised that, whatever might be the outcome of this enquiry into the death at her husband's establishment of a prominent official of the Central Government, there was bound to be unpleasantness. These modern officials, she reflected as she sat uncomfortably on the hard chair, did not understand the old customs of China – they had been brought up in the atmosphere of the Revolution of 1911, and judged things by very different standards.

" Ah Loo, or, to give him his full name, Loo Ching, you say, came to your house to see the girl Lien Fa, who has since disappeared ? " The Chief of Police eyed her severely.

" That is true," agreed the woman. " I wish it were not true."

" When did you last see Loo Ching alive ? "

She hesitated, and he was not slow to notice her

hesitation. " He came last to see her three days before this," she told him.

The pencil beat a tattoo on the blotting-pad. " I did not ask you when he came to see the girl. I asked when you saw him last."

" I did not understand you," she lied. " Loo Ching came to see me on the previous afternoon."

" On what business ? It could not have been on other grounds than business."

" He came to arrange about the proposed freedom of the girl Lien Fa," said Tung's wife. " He desired to take her into his house."

The Chief of Police sighed. " Alas, it seems that the proclamation of the Central Government has not reached your ears," he said. " Do you not know that all ownership of girls, formerly called the *mui-tsai* system, has passed, and that any girl who has, in the past, believed herself to be under compulsion to stop with her purchaser is free to go whither she will, by the decree of the Central Government ? "

" Rumours of this absurdity had reached me," the woman admitted, " but I did not believe them. For, if that were true, what would parents do with daughters whom they do not desire to keep ? Hitherto they have sold them to people in better financial circumstances."

" That is now illegal," Po Feng Hsi told her. " So the dead man saw you on the afternoon before, about purchasing the freedom of the girl Lien Fa.

Hw

Right. Now tell me, when did you hear of the murder ? ”

“ I was awakened by two of your policemen.”

“ You had not heard before ? Try to remember : any sound, a cry . . . ? ”

“ None,” answered Tung’s wife. “ I was asleep.”

“ Yes, that was reported to me. You were both asleep. Also, the telephone was standing on the table, as if someone had not had time to hang it on the hook of the instrument. Did you leave your telephone thus ? ”

“ I did not. I last telephoned to the *compradore*, late in the evening, for a supply of groceries.”

“ I see.” Po Feng Hsi sounded the little gong on the writing-desk. When the door opened, he said : “ Take this woman away. I may need to see her again. Now the serving-maid.”

When she came in, the little girl was frankly appalled. Her mouth hung open. Po Feng Hsi felt in his pocket and took out a couple of peanuts. “ There,” he said. “ Eat them.” He watched her, smiling, and by and by she began to feel more at ease. “Tell me what you know about Loo Ching.”

“ Loo Ching ? He used to come to see Lien Fa sometimes, and sometimes to see the noble lady Tung. He used to go into the lady’s room first, and then he would come and spend the night with Lien Fa. Many nights he came. We thought he was going to buy Lien Fa.”

“ Yes. And last night – did you see him ? ”

" I saw him come, and he was there with Lien Fa in her room.   Then they went to the room of the boy Ming So, and after a little, when I came back, I found the door locked.   Oh, yes, and the girl Yang Fei was in the same room with them.   With those two.   I do not think she was happy, but I do not know what was happening, because that is a door under which one cannot see.   That is all I know."

" You did not see them come out ? "

" I did not see them, because I went to sleep.   I often go to sleep, and the noble lady hits me.   But they must have come out, because . . ."

" Yes, yes.   I only want to know what you have seen.   Here is another peanut."   He struck the little gong, and the child went out, still munching.

Ming So stood very straight, facing Po Feng Hsi, a little overawed.

" You are the nephew of Tung Lai Luk ? " asked the Chief of Police.

" He is my uncle.   Yes."

" Tell me all you know."

Ming So coughed, as a man does when taking a deep breath.   Then he began : " I went to bed with the girl Yang Fei.   It is pleasant to sleep with a girl, I have discovered : it is thus possible to keep the feet warm without wrapping them up in cloth. When we woke, at dawn, I thought I had heard a noise, so I went to the next room, which was Yang Fei's room, and there, on the bed, I found the man, dead.   I know nothing more.   Oh, yes, I went to the bedroom of the noble lady Tung and telephoned to the police, very quietly, lest I should waken her and be beaten. She was not alone, so I expect she would have beaten me very hard. It is curious how many people seem to have discovered that which I told you – about keeping the feet warm in bed."

" Who was with her ? "

" I did not see who was with her. I was anxious to be silent, for I did not wish to be beaten, as I have already told you."

" And then ? "

" When I had telephoned, I went back to my own room."

The Chief of Police tapped again on his writing pad. " That is all very interesting, but it does not agree with the girl Yang Fei, who says that the man Loo Ching, came into her room, and that she killed him with the knife belonging to Lien Fa, which happened to be in her room. How do you account for that ? "

" Women imagine things," said the boy. " How could Loo Ching have come to see her, when she was sleeping with me ? How could she have killed him, when she was sleeping with me ? Why should she have killed him, as she says, if she was sleeping with me ? And why did the other girl, Lien Fa, run away, if it was not Lien Fa who killed Loo Ching ? " he ended triumphantly.

" These are questions," replied Po Feng Hsi, " which I prefer you to answer. Further, I might add to these questions this : where is your uncle, Tung Lai Luk ? What is this tale of brigands which I hear ? "

" My uncle was regrettably taken by brigands on the last day of our journey downriver from my family village of Ha Foo, and is now held for a ransom of ten thousand dollars. But I do not think that my aunt desires greatly that he should return to her bed, for she has made no effort, so far as I can discover, to gather the necessary money from his friends for his release. And in one moon from the time when they took my uncle away we have to be there, in the same place, with the ten thousand dollars, or the brigands will cut off portions – inconvenient portions – of my uncle."

" This is a strange tale," the Chief of Police protested. " It sounds to me very like the dreams of a boy who has idled too much."

" The tale may indeed be strange," countered Ming So, " but it is true. Ask of Yang Fei, whom he bought at the village of Seung So. Ask of the crew of the boat in which we travelled, who saw the brigands. You will find that this is not the sort of story which one imagines, but the truth."

" Very well." Po Feng Hsi smiled. " Now, you say that the girl Yang Fei could not have killed Loo Ching, as she says she did, because she was, all the night, in your bed."

" Yes, I said so. Is it likely that a man would let a woman go from his room before dawn ? It is towards dawn that the feet become coldest, and then it is that the woman becomes most needed. A bed is cold if one of the sleepers leaves it."

This time Po Feng Hsi laughed outright. "And are you so skilled in the arts of love, little one, that you can keep a woman with you all the night? Her tale seems to me the easier to credit."

" Does she dare to say," cried the boy, " that she was not with me? How false are women! At one moment they swear undying love, and at the next they have gone to another man, whom they desire – the gods know why – to murder. On her story, she should have equally desired to murder me, for I was the first to have her. Unless she denies altogether that she was with me at all, which is absurd."

" You may go now," the Chief of Police said, striking the gong. " And I would advise you to curb your imagination a little. When next I send for you, after you have had time for reflection, I shall expect to hear the truth."

" Expectation is poor food," muttered Ming So as he went out. Yang Fei passed him in the doorway, but she did not look at him.

" The little boy, Ming So, tells me that you were in his room until the dawn. Why did you not say so to me? " Po Feng Hsi asked her, when the door had been shut.

" I was ashamed," the girl answered. " He is so very young, and to a girl of sixteen . . ."

" But if you were with the boy, surely, as he says,

it is the boy whom you should have wished to murder, not Loo Ching, who was only second ? "

" The boy is only thirteen," she replied. " He is not yet a man."

" Now, tell me the whole truth." The Chief of Police suddenly put on his fiercest manner as he barked at her. " It will be better for you, and better for the boy. You do not desire me to suspect the boy of the murder, do you ? "

Her eyes opened wide. She was thrown off her balance by the unexpected and unanalysed possibility. Had she had time to think, she would have seen the absurdity of the suggestion, but, as it was, the story flowed from her, in halting sentences.

" That is all ? " asked Po Feng Hsi, when she had come to an end.

" That is all."

" You should have told the truth at once. Now go : you have nothing more to fear, nor has the boy Ming So. Report here " – he handed her an address – " and they will provide work for you. I shall telephone. Now go."

" But the boy . . ."

" The boy will be looked after. Go." He sat back in his chair and laughed as he sounded the gong again. The intrigues of children diverted him vastly. " Bring in the woman Tung," he ordered.

Tung's wife appeared far from happy when she came in the second time, for Po Feng Hsi wore the stern look of a man who has found out the truth.

" You are very fortunate," he said, " in not being put on trial for breaking the laws of the Republic. I have decided, this time, to overlook what you have done." The woman breathed more freely. " You may go. But remember that your establishment will be under suspicion for some time, and let discretion guide your footsteps. I have sent the girl Yang Fei to the new Government silk factory, where a post will be provided for her. As to your nephew, it is not for me to separate relations. But treat the boy with greater care than you have hitherto shown. A woman in whose house the son of the Minister of Public Works has been murdered cannot be too careful in the future. Now go. I do not think that the Minister, Loo Heng, will wish the matter pressed further. He has lost a son, but he has only himself to blame, since he did not bring up his son in the way of virtue. . . ." There came a knock at the door, and the entrance of an angry man. " Ah, Loo Heng, you received my message about your son's murder ? "

But the Minister of Public Works saw only the woman sitting opposite the desk.

" You ! " he said, and in a flash the Chief of Police understood many things.

After his first, unguarded expression of surprise, however, Loo Heng recovered himself. " I desire to know what steps are being taken," he demanded angrily, " to bring to justice the murderer of my son."

" While it grieves me," replied Po Feng Hsi, " to know that you have lost a son, my grief is moderated,

Loo Heng, by the knowledge that he was murdered at ' The Happy Heart ' by a girl, murdered in a fit of jealousy by a girl whom he was intending to purchase for his household. I think that you are fully aware how gravely our law now views such attempted but illegal bargains. The girl in question has disappeared, but of course the whole of the police force is at work on the problem of her whereabouts."

" You have not caught the murderess ? " Loo Heng found in vocal storming relief from the various questions which confronted him. But, even so, it was not easy to talk, with Tung Nan Tsz sitting there. " Please have this woman taken away. I do not thus wish to speak before strangers of the tragic loss which has befallen the family of Loo."

Smiling, Po Feng Hsi sounded the gong. Then he sat back in his chair listening to the stream of words from the Minister of Public Works. At a suitable moment he interrupted. " If you will excuse me for an instant, I have to telephone on urgent business." He went into another room to give orders for the employment of Yang Fei at the Government silk factory. When he returned, it appeared that Loo Heng's rage had evaporated, for he had departed.

.   .   .   .

" I am now aware of the truth of the matter, and I cannot but feel that it would have been better if you had told me that truth at once," the Chief of Police told Ming So. " It would have saved time. Nevertheless we must award credit where credit is deserved, and I confess that, in your place, I might have lied in the same way myself. Not that lying in general is to be encouraged. . . . Now, you will return to your aunt's house, and you will keep me informed of any unusual incidents which may occur there."

The boy objected. " I shall go and see Kung, my friend. He will, if I have judged him correctly, be able to find me other employment. I do not very much care to stay in the house of my uncle after what has happened. And, further, I must see what steps have to be taken in order to secure my uncle's release."

Po Feng Hsi nodded agreement. " You will no doubt, after this, act wisely. But this Kung of whom you speak : who is he ? "

" His name is Kung Hiao Ling, a man of great learning, who lives alone above the wine-shop at the junction of Market Street and Frog's Lane. He has many of the virtues of the Master, his ancestor."

" Then, both because he has those virtues and because he bears the most honoured name in China, you should not thus refer to him as ' Kung.' Say rather ' the honourable descendant of the Master.' However, I know of him, and, if he is content to listen to the babble of a small boy, you cannot do better than go to him for advice. You are wise. You may go now."

Again he sat back in his chair and laughed, thinking of the unrehearsed meeting of the Minister of Public Works with Tung's wife.

CHAPTER XIV

FUTURE AND PAST

THE little girl Pai Mei laid down the bunch of rice-plants and, having separated them, arranged them at suitable intervals along the line of the shallow trench where Ming Nai carefully planted each one with a deft motion of a stick and a final adjustment with her left hand.

" There are no more rice-plants than these," said Mei. " That was the last handful."

The older woman straightened her back. " That is good," she said. " It is hard work planting out rice, even with a helper such as you, my child."

" Do I not work quickly enough ? " asked Pai Mei. " I am sorry. Of course your son, Ming So, was quicker, but then he is a big boy, and strong."

" You are always thinking of my son Ming So," laughed his mother. " Be not so constant with your affections, for men always value most highly that which is not quite so certainly theirs. A too faithful wife, like an old pair of shoes, may be exchanged for another, just as new shoes, by their very squeaking, attract for the moment. Make men just a little doubtful. . . ."

" Have you heard more news ? " demanded the girl.

" No – I have heard nothing since the last letter,

of which I read you a part. I did not read all the letter to you, since there are some things which a girl of eleven should not hear, in the interests of herself."

" Tell me, mother," persisted the girl, and the courtesy title made the elder woman smile.

" No, my child : I will not tell you. It is not for you to know. When you are older, perhaps, I will tell you. Not now. But rest assured that he is not behaving unworthily of us. As to his uncle, I am not so sure, nor of his aunt," she added, as if in after-thought. " But all rests with Fate. I am not of those who go uselessly to the temple of Kwan Yin to pray the goddess to alter what Fate decrees. No – the sour with the sweet, the bright with the dark, I take them as they are sent. But it is not easy to keep the back straight under a burden."

" What has Ming So been doing ? " cajoled the girl, but without effect. Together they walked homewards in silence.

" I hope that the hire of the water-buffalo will be punctually paid," said Ming Nai suddenly. " It is not a satisfactory arrangement to hire out a beast without due payment." Then she paused and looked at Pai Mei in astonishment, forgetting the complaint she had been about to make against a neighbour whom she did not trust too greatly where money was concerned, for she saw that, for once in a way, Pai Mei had not been listening to her.

" May I go out this evening ? " Mei asked innocently, and Ming Nai nodded permission. How absorbed in their own thoughts children were, she reflected as they walked homewards.

.   .   .   .

Thus it came about that the girl Pai Mei reached the pool below the waterfall just while daylight lasted. It was lonely here, with no answering voice anywhere, and somehow even the accustomed noises of the forest around her were stilled, so that only the continual hiss and purr of the waterfall sounded as she stepped silently into the pool and waded out to the middle of the sheet of water. The moon stood just under the fringe of the forest, and the curtain of falling water hung, luminous, it seemed, with the smooth green edge like a bar of green where the water appeared to hesitate before finally plunging to the froth below.

" Oh, Kwan Yin, Kwan Yin, Mother of Mercy," cried the child, as she stood, breast-deep, facing the waterfall, " turn eyes of pity on me and on him. Keep foremost in his memory, in his dreams, the moment which we spent here together, so that, remembering, he may remain mine. Hear, O Mother of Mercy ; hear." No echo came amongst the faint sighing of the wind in the high trees and the noisy plashing of the water. " O divine Goddess, who carest specially for women, care for me. Make him love always what he loved once, here, in this place. O Thou who inhabitest no temple willingly, Thou who amidst the chants of priests cannot hear clearly the prayers of Thy worshippers, hear me now, in this free place, where Thou and I meet, Goddess, once only, as he and I met once only in the same place. For all else was but a seeming – here was truth, when he held me in his arms, here, in this pool, and the moon – Thy moon, Goddess – crept up as it creeps now above the edges of the trees. . . ."

But Pai Mei did not finish her prayer to Kwan Yin, for the words dried in her throat as she gazed at the waterfall. Half way down the sheet of dim radiance appeared an area of black, and below this area the waters no longer poured down in a stream. Then the black was gone ! and again the clear, unbroken surface of white, falling water stretched from the smooth green edge above to white foam below.

The girl did not analyse her feelings, seeking to classify the occurrence as a sign, a portent, or an answer to her prayers. She waded on towards the waterfall, shoulder-high now, then found the bottom of the pool rising again. Before her stretched the vertical face of the fall, and she walked into it blindly, eyes shut. The roar in her ears ceased, and she opened her eyes again.

Behind the barrier through which she had just passed a cave ran back into the bank. There was no light in this cave except such of the fast-departing twilight as passed through the curtain of water, but in the cave were rude comforts. A jug of water, still dripping, stood by the wall : this had been, she saw now, the object protruding for a moment from the waterfall. On a pile of rugs sat a man who seemed to the startled child of incredible age, for his white beard reached, as he sat, to the floor by his side. He was sitting quite motionless, looking straight in front of him.

Pai Mei was so surprised that she forgot to cry out. But as she half turned the old man said : " Come here." Then, as she stepped backwards, away from him : " I am an old man, and blind, but my ears tell me that you have come. And your breathing is as the breathing of something young. More I cannot tell, save that you are frightened. Are you boy or girl ? "

He did not move from his position, and with the ceasing of his thin voice it seemed that the noisy cave was silent.

" I am a boy, and my name is Ming So," said Pai Mei. " I was swimming in the pool . . ."

" Climb up to the floor of the cave and come here," said the old man. " Sit down opposite to me, there. I shall not touch you : you need not be afraid." His ears seemed to follow her slightest movement with exactness. " A boy – Ming So. That is strange. Well, why do you come to me ? Few come to me now, for few can find me here. Do you seek to know the future ? "

" I was swimming in the pool," began the girl again.

" I have heard that. Ah, well it is good for the young to be shy. You would like to see the future, but you dare not ask. I will show you the past, then. The past is less terrifying to the young. By now the twilight should have passed to night, and the curtain before us is a just visible grey. On this curtain of falling water, maybe, you shall see the past of Ming So."

He turned to his left as he sat.

" On the curtain appears a room, such a room as boy may occupy in a city," the thin voice went on. " That is strange, for it is many days' journey to the city. On the bed – which is a high bed, unlike the beds which are usual in China, as you know – on this bed sits a boy. He is thirteen years old. By his side there sits another, a girl a little older. There is no light in the room. She pulls him towards her and pillows his head on her lap while she tells him old poetry, so that after a little while he sleeps. It is very hot in the room, for they are not clothed. Now a noise sounds at the door . . ."

" Stop ! " cried Pai Mei. " Do not speak thus. It is not true."

The old man laughed – a thin crackling laugh like bamboos in a south wind. " No more of the past, then, since you say it is not true, but the future. Lo, the same boy, very little older, is sitting by a fire on open ground. Above him the stars move slowly across a velvet sky. The fire flickers, and brightens with strange, moving tongues the faces of those who sit with the boy round the fire under the circling stars."

"I am not Ming So," said Pai Mei, crying quietly. "I am Pai Mei, a foolish girl who loves that Ming So."

The picture on the waterfall had vanished.

"Many girls used to say that in the days when girls came to see me," said the old man. "I knew that you were not a boy, for a boy does not pray to Kwan Yin. But be comforted : I am a very old man, and I cannot see you now as you sit there, I suppose, with the last gleam of a light that has already gone lighting the curves which Ming So, one day, will delight again to see and to honour. For boys and men worship at no such altar as you, my child. For them beauty, fleeting beauty, is the goddess behind the veil, and while that beauty lasts they worship. But you are crying again – I hear you. Be comforted – you are yet young ; the years have not yet rubbed into a smudge the lines of your body."

"I must go," whispered the girl. "It is not right to talk to you thus, with no clothes."

"I am an old man with keen ears," he answered, "and you are but a child. There is no harm. See, my evening meal has come. Ah, I forgot, you cannot see in the dark. But here is the otter who brings my fish. Listen : he bites, ever so gently, at the back of the head, so that now the gleaming body lies still, here, at my feet. Come : I will cook it for us both."

She heard him rise to his feet, and from a corner came the sound of flint on steel, then a tiny flicker of flame. She saw now that he held in his hand a large

Iw

fish, and as the flame flared up a dark, shiny body slid over into the water. The otter had gone.

" He is always afraid of the fire," said the old man, echoing her thoughts. " Like me, he prefers the night. There, the fish is cooking. Child, you shiver : I can hear your teeth rattling. Come to the fire and warm yourself."

The fire which he had lit on the rock floor blazed up, but Pai Mei dashed through the waterfall and waded ashore, still sobbing. The waterfall showed with all the colours of the rainbow as she looked at it, and Pai Mei remembered that rainbows represented the not at all respectable love-affairs of the Ying and the Yang, whereby the world was first brought into being. . . . She fled into the kindly tunnel of the forest, grasping her clothes, running as if pursued.

But there were no pursuers save her own thoughts – the picture of Ming So sleeping in the lap of another girl. . . .

CHAPTER XV

THEIR STRENGTH IS TO SIT STILL

" If you think that it would be better for me to remain in the house of Tung, I will do so," said Ming
So, sitting very upright opposite Kung Hiao Ling
in the big room above the wine-shop at the junction
of Frog's Lane and Market Street. " It will be
difficult to behave with the dignity becoming to a
man after what has happened, since everyone in
' The Happy Heart ' will be aware that I was
stripped of my clothes and made to endure indigni-
ties which I cannot contemplate without shivering.
But if you think that it would be wise for me to
remain . . ."

" I do think so," said Kung. " Since you are an
intelligent boy, I will tell you why I think that it
would be wise for you to do so. You see, without
your presence at ' The Happy Heart ' we have no
one there on whom we can rely for information.
The girl Yang has gone to the Government silk
factory, the child who serves meals and sweeps is too
young to know how to observe and how not to
observe. . . ."

" But," objected Ming So, " you know all about
the household – much more than I have told you.
How is this ? "

Kung Hiao Ling smiled. " I know from my own

enquiries, from the information which Po, the Chief of Police, gave me this morning, and also from what you have not said."

"From what I have not said? I do not understand, sir."

"To a wise man what you do not say is just as valuable for information as what you do say. But have I advanced reasons enough for your remaining at the house of Tung?"

"Your advice waits on no reasons," said Ming So. "I shall remain there. Would it be possible for me to hear some of the things which you have found out?"

"Bring me that wine-jar and fill my cup. Now, the first interesting thing is the disappearance of your uncle. You remember that you told me how quietly the brigands came to take him away? There was no shooting, no blood – only a quiet order and a quiet compliance with that order. Of course, in the face of superior force it is useless to struggle, but still . . . Think on that fact. Then, secondly, there is the behaviour of Tung's wife, Tung Nan Tsz, your aunt. Not only does she make no effort to gather money from her friends, as I have ascertained, but she exhibits a friendship for Loo Heng which is peculiar when you consider that he is the Minister of Public Works, and that his son was also employed in the same office, while she follows a trade which, however ancient it may be, is hardly one where we hope to find Government officials involved."

" Involved ? " queried Ming So.

" Involved. There was more in their acquaintance than her business justified. I think that I know what it was, but I will not tell you yet."

" I do not question your wisdom," said the boy. " But when, honourable sir, is the money to be raised for my uncle's ransom ? For, in spite of his wife's behaviour, and in spite of what I have endured at ' The Happy Heart,' I still feel it to be my duty to try to rescue him from the consequences of his journeying on my behalf."

" Do not distress yourself on that account," Kung smiled. " I shall see to it. And you will not regard my promise as an empty one. But remember that, if I appear to do nothing, if Tung Nan Tsz does nothing, you will not protest. You will just watch and report to me. Do you understand ? "

" I understand. I will do as you say. But I do not think that my aunt likes me, after what has occurred. It will be awkward if she takes it into her head to turn me from the door."

" She cannot do that, since her absent husband wished you to be there. And, however I may doubt her real desire to do her husband's will, I am sure that, outwardly, she will show you the same care as he would have done. She knows the value of appearances. You will, in any case, take the precaution of being on your guard and reporting to me any incidents which may seem strange to you."

" I will. Now I must go. I have been away much longer than it needs to post a letter, and I wish to give rise to no suspicion."

" Good," smiled Kung. " Fill my cup before you depart."

Chapter XVI

AN OLD FAIRY-TALE

MING NAI laid a cool hand on the child's feverish brow. " Now, Mei, lie still, like a good girl, and perhaps I will tell you one of the old stories. Then you will sleep, and the fever will pass."

" I shall die, and Ming So will not know that I am dead," wailed Pai Mei.

" No – you will not die ; do not be so foolish. Would Ming So wish you thus to sadden his mother by talking of death ? Besides, it is silly. You are too much of a nuisance, Mei, to die while you are young. Wait until you are more useful – that is the time to die. Now, what story would you like ? The story of the weaver-girl, or of the monkey who argued with Buddha, or . . . "

" Is there a story," whispered the girl, " of an old man who lives behind a waterfall and tells you the past and the future ? "

" There is such a story. Now, I wonder where you heard that ? Lie back, put your hands under the bedclothes, and listen. Once upon a time there was a girl who loved deeply a prince whom she had once met. She had only seen him once, and had not even spoken to him, so that I was wrong to say ' met.' She hoped that this prince loved her, too, and all the days when she was in the fields, or working in

135

the house, her thoughts were made happy by the hope of his love. For boys and girls, you know, think love to be something very different from that habit of living together which older people find it. Put your hands under the clothes."

" They loved each other," said Pai Mei, rapt. " Go on."

" Well, the girl one day went to the river to bathe, and while she was bathing – quite alone, of course – she found a waterfall below a cliff of green jade. Being a curious girl, she ventured to pass through the waterfall, and on the far side of it she found an old man, blind as a mole, but . . ."

" I know," whispered Pai Mei. " He had a long white beard and lived on fish which the otter brought to him."

" Since you appear to know this story, shall I tell you another one ? "

" No – tell me about the old man."

" Well, she was surprised to see him, sitting thus behind a waterfall, but, since he was blind, she did not feel that she need withdraw. So she told him that she was a boy – you know that the voices of young boys and girls are much the same – and gave the name of the prince whom she loved, as if it were her own."

" Is this a story ? " asked the girl in bed.

" Of course this is a story ! Do you think that I am telling you something that happened to me ? Why, I cannot swim. Shall I go on ? "

" Please," said Pai Mei.

" She told him that she was the prince, and he showed her the past and the future, not of herself, but of the prince. And when she saw what the past of the prince was like, she hated the prince, and when she saw what the future of the prince was like, she hated him still more, and she . . ."

" That is not true," interrupted Pai Mei. " She did not hate him. Oh, my head burns ! Give me a drink of water and tell me another story."

" You have not let me finish the first, and tell you how it was all a mistake, and how they lived happily ever afterwards when the prince returned and told her the truth of the things which she had heard from the old man behind the waterfall. But I will give you more water. Here."

" They lived happily ever afterwards ? " asked Pai Mei, and her eyes were bright.

" Yes, of course. They always do live happily ever afterwards in these old stories. It is only in the new stories that the ending is not happy."

" I like the old stories better," said Pai Mei, snuggling down and closing her eyes. " I shall get better now. I do not any longer want to die."

Ming Nai softly stepped away and left her sleeping.

CHAPTER XVII

NEWS AND A DREAM

THE boy Ming So had struck up with the porter of
" The Happy Heart " that species of friendship
which is always possible between those whose
stations in life are markedly different. Ming found
in the porter's keen, cynical sense of humour a
dryness which fitted well with the development of
his adolescent mind, while the porter not only liked
displaying for the boy's benefit such gems of wit as
he possessed, but also felt that, in thus hob-nobbing
with the powers above him, he was rendering more
secure his own tenure of his post. The two would sit
side by side in the entrance-hall, passing not always
inaudible comments on the patrons of the establishment as they came and went.

This acquaintance, from Ming So's point of view,
possessed a further advantage, in that from his
friend the porter he learned just the gossip which he
was expected daily to serve up to the noble lady
Tung, and gossip, at that, which she could always
verify, if she so desired, without the danger of her
finding that the boy had drawn too deeply on his
imagination. The two were sitting thus one late
afternoon some three weeks after Ming So's arrival
at " The Happy Heart " when a man came with a
letter. This man was clearly not of the city, and to

the boy, as he sat there only half interested, there seemed something familiar in the set of the man's shoulders, the line of the back of his head. . . .

" I will leave you here," said the porter, " in charge, while I take this doubtless unimportant letter to the noble lady Tung. It would not be fitting to leave unguarded the entrance to so many delights."

Ming So nodded. He was watching the departing back of the man who had brought the letter. Then he suddenly remembered with a start. Of course – this was the bearer of the lantern who had accompanied the leader of the pirates when Uncle Tung Lai Luk had fallen into the hands of those desperate men ! And the man had gone, and it might be impossible to find him again. . . . The boy sprang to his feet and ran out into the street, leaving the many delights of which the porter had spoken to look after themselves. He ran, and as he reached the end of the street he sighted his quarry, hastening back, presumably, to the wharf. . . . Ming dropped to a walk, thinking hard. It would be of no avail to make a scene, for no one would believe a boy. So he followed, and by the time that the river came into sight he had made up his mind. He would follow this man to the place where they were keeping his uncle, and would try to set his uncle free.

The messenger went on board one of the many boats in the river, and Ming hung about in the twilight, watching for signs of the boat's departure. He knew that most boats were towed up the river

by steamers for as great a distance as this means of
transport was possible : where the river became
impassable for steam, reliance had to be placed on
the ancient method of man-power. The boy's quick
eye noted that a launch in the vicinity had steam up,
while all round, on all the boats near him, streams
of coolies bore barrels, sacks, bundles, and cases
down to the waiting craft. On the boat in which
he was particularly interested, Ming So noted, white
wood barrels were stacked high on the deck. He
followed with his eye to the high pile of these same
barrels standing near him on the wharf. Their
contents were easy to identify, for from the barrels
rose a strong, persistent odour of dried fish.

Instantly the problem solved itself. He waited
his opportunity and then, when no one was looking,
tipped three-quarters of the contents of the nearest
barrel out into the slimy water at the back of the
floating wharf, climbed into the barrel, and arranged
the lid in place just as he heard approaching him
the voices of the coolies. And then, after a jerky,
sick journey and eventual arrival at his destination
on the deck, he remembered what he ought to have
remembered before – that the convoy could not
start before daylight, in any case.

After dark, therefore, a small figure might have
been seen creeping into " The Happy Heart," and
behind the figure remained, as he passed, an
unmistakable odour of dried fish.

Ming went to bed early. The next morning, long

before dawn, he proposed taking his place again in his barrel of dried fish in pursuit of his knightly adventure.

.   .   .   .

The tattoo of finger-nails sounded on Ming So's bedroom door, and he got up to open it. Yang Fei came into the room, and he was astonished to note the difference in the girl. No longer was she the oppressed, unhappy child, for she had apparently spent her first three weeks' pay from the Government silk factory almost entirely on clothes. He stood gazing in astonishment at the radiant personality before him.

" May I come in ? " asked Yang Fei, having come in. " I came to bring you good news." She shut the door behind her.

" Good news is best in daylight," returned the boy. " But go on, since you are here."

" It is that the things which happened to me when I lived here have had no ill effect."

" I do not understand you," said Ming So. " Have you come here, and at this hour, to tell me that you are in good health ? "

She dropped her eyes. " In a sense, yes. For in the mouth of a girl good news means more than in the mouth of a boy."

" I still do not understand. Must you propound puzzles when I have gone to bed ? Speak plainly."

" I am not going to have a baby," she said. " I thought that you would understand."

" And who," he demanded, " ever thought that you were going to have a baby ? People only have babies when they are married, and you are not married, so how could you have a baby ? "

She smiled at his ignorance. " No, little Ming So, I am not married. One day you will understand more clearly what I have just told you, and you will know, also, the reason for my great joy."

" It seems to me that all this talk about knowing if you are going to have a baby is all dog's wind," said Ming So, for he was annoyed. " How can one tell, and why should one expect such things ? "

" You will know one day," she repeated. " But you should be flattered that I came, first, to tell you, because it was your presence that made me endure what I did endure. When I remember " – and she put her arm round him – " my vision of a figure with a long dagger, striking again and again at the back of the man with whom I had slept, I am still cold with fear. But now . . ."

" But you knew it was Lien Fa," he said. " That would make it less horrible. And, in any case, you would do well to forget it and let me go to bed. Was it not Lien Fa whom you saw ? "

" Of course it was. Who else could it have been ? But, to see in my memory the long knife, rising and falling . . ." She buried her head on his shoulder.

" Oh, yes, you may stop if you like," grumbled the boy. " If you want to. But I have to go out very early, before dawn, on important business, so do not

wake me again in the night with your tales of
murders, and knowing whether a girl is going to
have a baby or not. Now, good night ; we have
talked enough. And if you wake at dawn and I am
still here, wake me, for I shall have overslept. But I
think that I shall have wakened first." He turned his
back and went to sleep.

Yang Fei lay down beside him. Then, after a
minute, she rose again and moved about the room.
Suddenly she found the object of her search, and,
opening the window, jammed under it the fishy
garments which Ming So had discarded on the floor,
so that they hung down outside the window in the
open air. Then she lay down again.

.   .   .   .

In the deep violet sky of Ming So's dream, rather
larger stars than one would have expected were
fixed like Catherine wheels at arbitrary points in the
heavens. Like Catherine wheels, too, they seemed
to be revolving slowly, so that streaks and lines of
light emanating from them crossed and recrossed
like the rays of a battery of lighthouses.

There was no moon in his dream, but scattered
through the sky the boy saw long, cylindrical fragments of translucent material, like milk-glass, aim-
lessly drifting.

And now, on one of these fragments near the
horizon, he detected a seated figure. As she drew
nearer, he saw that Pai Mei was sitting astride a
bundle of these translucent cylinders, tied together

with string, of nearly but not quite equal lengths. She sat upright, as one sits a horse, and her left arm was held, slightly curved, above her head, like a circus rider's when a jump has been safely negotiated.

The bundle of moonbeams which bore Pai Mei came towards him, hovered gently, and as gently descended to earth, leaving the little girl standing astride above it as it lay on the ground with a faint, bluish vapour ascending from it.

" I have come," said Pai Mei, and gave a kick to the large, flabby fish on which she had been riding, it appeared. The fish bent somewhat in the middle as it slithered across the floor away from them. She must have hurt her toes, kicking the fish like that, Ming reflected, for she wore no shoes, nor, indeed, did she wear anything at all, though she seemed very properly unconscious of the fact.

" What were you doing ? " Pai Mei asked.

Now Ming So turned, following the direction of her pointing finger, towards the bed where Yang Fei still slept solidly on her face, one arm up, pillowing her head.

" That is my own affair," he replied, in his dream.

" It is mine also," said Pai Mei, pointing again to the large, flabby fish lying there on the bed. " It appears to be a very strange thing to do, thus to go to bed with a fish, and with such a large fish, too."

" It is not my fault," answered the boy. " I asked for lobsters, but they gave me this. They told me that it was more reliable than lobsters."

" And *does one climb a tree to seek for fish* ? "
came now the voice of his mother, Ming Nai.
" And to climb on such a tall bed as this in order to
search for lobsters seems to be not quite what I
should have expected."

Pai Mei had shrunk now to about half size, holding
his hand as she stood there. The lobsters had
gathered in a ring about them both and were closing
in. He recognised amongst these lobsters several of
the girls whom he had spoken to at " The Happy
Heart." They, of course, wore no clothes either,
nor did he. . . .

Ming So woke up in a cold sweat of fear. He knew
that he felt, even without looking at the girl sleeping
there in his bed, quite different from anything
which he had ever felt before, and that he was very
much afraid. His teeth wanted to chatter, although
he was not cold. . . .

He slipped out of bed and, after much searching,
found the garments which Yang Fei had hung outside the window. When he was dressed he felt
better, safer, but even now the strange sensation of
his dream was long in leaving him. He looked down
at the sleeping Yang Fei, and then hurriedly looked
away again, for looking at Yang Fei seemed to make
this sensation worse again. It was all most disturbing.

Opening the door softly, he fled on silent feet
down empty corridors (for it was near the dawn)
to the street, and so back to the barrel of dried fish
on the launch tied up at the wharf.

Kw

Chapter XVIII

THE LITERARY METHOD

" AND that is the result of my enquiries into the boy's disappearance," said the Chief of Police. " He was last seen by the porter, giving evidence of his discreet methods of life, for he was then going up to bed at the hour of ten. The only evidence which I have not heard is evidence which I wished you, Kung, to hear with me – that of the girl Yang Fei. I have her waiting below."

Kung Hiao Ling smiled and replenished his wine-cup. " You will drink another cup before she comes ? " he asked. "No ? What a pity ! For I have chosen of all the vices the least harmful to others : a man may sit and drink until he is one with the dwellers in the moon, and if he still sits thereafter he is no trouble to anyone else. Did not the poet say . . ."

" I hesitate to forgo the pleasure of hearing from you what the poet said," observed Po Feng Hsi, " but I would remind you that while you drink the world goes on turning, and time is not wholly unimportant where the disappearance of Ming So is our concern. Shall I have the girl brought up to speak with us ? "

Kung nodded. " Do what you will. I cannot expect all men, however they may be wise in other ways, to see things from my own angle. Yes, call her."

The other struck a gong. To the Chinese detective who appeared he said : " The girl."

" I think," observed the drinker, " that the modern craze for shortness of speech is carried to excess. To use two words where there is legitimate use for a sentence – to use a sentence where a speech is requisite – appears to me . . ."

Yang Fei entered and stood before the two men.

" Tell your story," said the Chief of Police.

" Nay, not so curtly, elder-born," protested Kung. " Rather, my young friend, bearer of the name of the famous concubine of the Emperor Huang, tell us, if you will, of the events of last night, when you entered again the house of ' The Happy Heart,' leaving again at an early hour to-day. For on what you say much depends."

" That is what I said," objected Po Feng Hsi, but the girl had already begun her tale.

" I went to see Ming So," she said, " and found him in bed. He was tired, and I stayed with him."

" Unusual, but kind," commented Kung, choosing words which were some two centuries out of date, just to annoy the Chief of Police.

" Before he went to sleep he told me that he was compelled to go out on business before dawn, and commanded me, if he was still sleeping at dawn, to wake him. But I slept, and when I woke he had gone. So I, too, left ' The Happy Heart ' and went to have my rice before beginning work at the factory. That is all I know."

Kung refilled his cup. " That is a collection of facts," he said, "such as you, Po Feng Hsi, delight to hear. For my part, I prefer the subtler information which the spirit gives – the airs that breathe upon the mind from unnoticed objects, the scent of a blossom round the corner."

" Valuable as literature, but valueless as evidence," said the Chief of Police. Then he smiled at the girl. " Did you, then, experience these soul-disturbing emanations of which the cultured Kung speaks ? "

Yang Fei, after all, knew " The Everlasting Wrong," and resented the criticism which she felt in the voice of the Chief of Police.

" It is unfitting," she said, " to jeer at literature and the *unusual but kind* remarks of the descendant of the Master. Besides, he is right." She employed Kung's own pair of adjectives.

" Explain," said the Chief of Police, ignoring her implication.

" He spoke of airs, of scent. There was a smell, which I have just recollected – a smell of dried fish." When the two men had finished laughing, she went on. " It was a suit of the boy's clothes. I hung them out of the window to air, and when I woke to find him gone, the clothes and the smell had gone, too."

" Dried fish ? " mused the Chief of Police, looking at Kung.

" Dried fish," Kung answered jestingly. " Can you read the riddle ? Has the emanation of which you spoke disturbed the soul of which you also spoke, O Chief of Wordless Police ? "

" The methods of the literary artist are beyond my understanding, elder-born. Would you deign to explain to me ? "

Kung rang the gong. When the detective reappeared, he said : " Telephone to the police office at the city wharf and ascertain the destination of a large cargo of dried fish which was sent off yesterday." Then he refilled his wine-cup. " Also, find out from the man who was posted to watch ' The Happy Heart ' if a countryman came the day before, probably with a letter, for the noble lady Tung. When these answers have come, Po Feng Hsi, we can go on with our plans."

" Your plans," replied the Chief of Police, smiling.

" Our plans. I dream ; you translate into action ; which is, after all, the peculiar duty and privilege of a policeman. Girl, if I may be short with you, will you go downstairs and wait until something has happened ? Then we will send for you. Po, a cup of wine now ? "

" While waiting, I have no objection to, perhaps, one cup," answered the Chief of Police.

.   .   .   .

Later, the detective returned.

" Well," asked Po Feng Hsi.

" The fish was destined for one day's journey up-river. The countryman to whom you referred arrived late in the afternoon and left again immediately. It is not known for whom the letter was designed, but it was given to the woman Tung. After the countryman had left, the boy Ming So also left, but returned in the evening."

" I bow to your incredible perspicacity," said the Chief of Police to Kung Hiao Ling. " What now ? "

" The detective may return to his detection," said Kung. " You and I will explain to this girl what is required of her."

" I did not know that anything was required," said the other.

" Much is required, including intelligence," replied Kung. " I have hopes, too, that she may possess intelligence, for she shows an appreciation of literature."

" I bow again," replied the Chief of Police, as he prepared to listen.

.   .   .   .

" I am going away for a holiday," said Kung, when he had finished telling the Chief of Police what was to be done. " I shall go up-river, alone. Do not fail to act as I have suggested, and if, in my absence, any new question of policy should arise, reflect, before you make your decision, that action, admirable as it is, marks a man who has not taken sufficient time to

NOEL
SYERS.

" *I bow again*," replied the Chief
of Police, as he prepared to listen

think. It is better not to act at all than to act unwisely."

" I will strive to graft the bough of your method on
the tree of my own," replied Po Feng Hsi, a trifle
doubtfully, as he prepared to depart. " It will be
difficult, for I have been learning to rely on you.
Must you take a holiday just now ? "

" Yes : I have heard of a new vintage of wine, and
I go to seek it," Kung announced.

Chapter XIX

SLEUTH

YANG FEI stood with bowed head in front of the wife of Tung Lai Luk.

" That was my wish," she said. " It occurred to me that since Lien Fa had gone away, you would have space for one more girl, and I had the temerity to hope that . . ."

" And how about your price ? " asked Tung's wife. " I am not prepared to pay much."

" My qualifications are so small," replied the girl, " that I should not dream of asking more than a small amount. And, after all, the payment which was made to my father by your honourable husband really answers the question. Still, if you would open for me a banking account and pay in what you think right each month, I shall not complain."

" It is an easy life," said Tung's wife. " Foolish girls are they who labour long hours in a factory when it is possible for them to live here in ease and comfort. The Government is very foolish, too, in desiring to abolish or alter the bargains made by a parent. It is not in consonance with the ancient custom of our race."

" Yes, they should not interfere with the bargains made by a parent," said Yang Fei. " Now, if you will excuse me, I will go to fetch my property from the room which I have been renting near the Government silk factory."

" Go, then : I wish more girls were as sensible as you appear to be," said Tung's wife ; and, when Yang Fei had shut the door after her, Tung's wife sat for a long time, resting her head on her hands, thinking. . . .

Later, Yang Fei called the little sewing-maid into her room. " Child," she said, " do you like sweet-meats ? Such as this ? " A small hand accepted the sticky offering. " What is your name ? "

" My name," said the child, " I do not know. That is to say that everyone calls me, *mui*, which just means ' girl,' and I do not remember ever having had any other name. But I must carry these bowls of rice to the room of the noble lady. Do all other girls have names ? "

" Most of them," said Yang Fei. " But we must see about getting you a name. Perhaps the noble lady knows your name. Now you must go and proceed with your duties, as you were doing before I asked you in here to give you a sweetmeat."

Beneath the bedroom door she saw that the shadows of two feet moved swiftly away.

.   .   .   .

Three o'clock in the morning, with clouds obscur-ing all but the glimmer of a light from the sky. Behind Yang Fei, as she shut the door, lay the dark corridor, empty save for little rustlings – a yawn, a sigh, a creak. Before her, under the small light, the bedroom of Tung's wife showed mysteriously dark in the corners. The girl tiptoed over to the bed, to make sure that the occupants slept as soundly as the sleeping-draught, which she had slipped into their rice while the small servant was not looking, led her to expect. It was curious to see the man – Loo Heng, the Minister of Public Works – lying asleep there with his foolish mouth open and his lips dry and shining faintly, while beside him the woman lay on her face with one arm on the pillow and the other resting across the chest of the sleeping Loo. Presumably they loved each other in some sort of way, these two. And Yang Fei suddenly drew her mind back from a consideration of the ethics of the position, as she remembered what she had come for.

The papers on the table were bills only – bills and receipts. Yang Fei drew from an inner pocket the little piece of wire with which the Chief of Police had spent half an hour teaching her to open all the locks in Kung's room, and put on her hands a pair of rubber gloves. . . . The drawers contained clothing, medicine, articles of which she could only guess the use, until she finally opened the last in the lacquer cabinet. Here were letters, and she scanned them one by one. Only three down she found what she had been seeking, and, without reading the whole of it, slipped the letter into her pocket and carefully relocked the drawer with her piece of wire. Then she gave a last look at the sleepers and returned to her own room.

Locking herself in, she took a reel of cotton from her pocket, tied the end to a nail in the window-frame, and released the reel as far as she could reach over the sill, in the direction of the stream below. For a little while nothing further happened : then her hand felt tugs on the cotton – two long and one short tug – again two long and one short. She took the rubber gloves from her pocket, inserted in one of them the rolled-up letter, slipped the second glove over the first, and twisted the whole into a bundle, which she secured with the piece of wire which the Chief of Police had given her. Through the ring on the end of this wire she inserted the end of the cotton which she still held, and then, leaning out from the window, let the package fall towards the ground below.

She waited, cotton over her finger, like a fisherman waiting for a bite. By and by came a new series of pulls on the cotton – two short and one long – and she threw clear her end of the cotton, shut the window noiselessly, and lay down to sleep.

Chapter XX

DRIED FISH

MING So was glad to observe, under the partially raised lid of the barrel, that a long overdue twilight was approaching. He was cramped from squatting on his haunches in the barrel throughout the long hours of the boat's passage upstream : the evil juice of the fish had penetrated his shoes : the sausage which he had hurriedly put in his pocket the night before tasted of fish : his hair seemed greasier than usual.

Thus it was with delight that he found the boat drawn to a wharf just as the lanterns at various mast-heads began to throw circles of light on wet decks, and discovered that he could, in the comparative darkness of his part of the boat, slip unobserved from his unpleasant hiding-place and take cover on the wharf.

The man whom he had been following was last to go ashore. Ming stood in the shadow of the pile of cases on the wharf, then slid silently in the direction which the man had taken.

His quarry passed through the village of Nam Pa and set out along a narrow road between paddy-fields. The boy felt at home here, and took advantage of this feeling to have a quick drink from a tethered water-buffalo which some farmer had not yet fetched in for the evening milking. Even so, the buffalo-milk tasted unpleasantly of fish.

He followed the man into the country. On both sides the paddy-fields seemed to recede in infinite areas of wet mud : then the two came to the end of the paddy-fields, and Ming plodded on, ever at a safe distance behind the heels of the other, into the open country by a track which hardly earned the name of road. He was half asleep with fatigue, but still he hung on grimly to the man in front, conscious that he was only doing what he conceived to be his duty. By and by he saw a light ahead of them : he moved nearer – as near as safety permitted. The man entered the courtyard of a house : Ming followed.

In the warm night two people were sitting out under the gleam of coloured paper lanterns hung on poles stuck into the ground. And Ming So, listening to their talk, was surprised to see that the man whom he had followed went up to one of these figures and said : " I presented your letter to the wife of Tung Lai Luk, and then I came away at once, without waiting for a reply, as you commanded."

" Good," said a second voice. " Go now ; that is all. My daughter, tell me what you have been saying about old Tung Lai Luk. I fear that I have been half asleep in this twilight."

Lien Fa's familiar voice replied.

" Tung could not get a mortgage on his business, because his own bank knows that the Government

intends shortly to make all such businesses illegal,
and then they will have no value on which a
bank would give a mortgage. But his wife knows
Loo Heng, the Minister of Public Works, who is,
also, a director of her bank – of the lady Tung's
bank, I mean. So it is possible that, with sympathy
from her friends and influence from Loo Heng, she
may succeed in getting her mortgage. She certainly would not have got it if Tung himself had
been in Kwei Sek, because Tung is jealous of Loo
Heng, and does not allow him to come to the
house."

A third figure came towards them.

" Still talking ? " came the voice of Tung Lai
Luk. " Lien Fa, what is this smell of fish which
affronts me ? "

Ming So could not get out of the courtyard unnoticed, so he took his courage in both hands.

" I have come to share your confinement, my
uncle," he said. " I regret that, on the way, I fell
into contact with certain cargo on the boat by which
I came. . . ."

" Lien Fa, take the boy away and wash him,"
said Tung. " Wash him thoroughly. Ha, you
laugh, do you ? " he said to the brigand. " Lien
Fa will enjoy the task, if I know her. Always seeking the company of the young of the sex, that was
ever her motto. Now – what about a game of Ma
Jongg ? We can get the other two, when the boy
has been washed. . . ."

Ming So, amazed at the treatment which his uncle seemed to be receiving at the hands of these unexpectedly kindly brigands, was led away by The Lily.

" But," he said, when she had taken him to a pump at the other side of the house, " I do not understand at all. Why are you here, and why does the brigand treat my uncle with such unbrigandish courtesy ? "

The girl laughed at him. " You will understand soon enough, little curious one. Now – take off all those evil-smelling garments, every one of them, and give them to me. I will fetch such of my own clothes as you can wear. Hurry ! Tung Lai Luk desires to play Ma Jongg with us, and we must not be too long, or he will get in a bad temper. Come, hurry ! It is getting dark here, or I would help you myself."

" I prefer," returned Ming So, stripping off the odorous garments, " to be my own valet. I seem to remember another occasion on which you made the same offer, but more forcibly." He held out a collection of garments. " Stay – there are more, Lien Fa. It is indeed a strange whim on the part of the eternal gods that I should so often be naked. I think that, had the gods in question considered the matter at all, they would have arranged for man to be feathered. Here are the other clothes. Take them and return swiftly with garments to replace them."

" While I am gone," said Lien Fa, " wash under

this pump, and wash thoroughly, for you smell of fish more than I had imagined anything other than a fish could smell. I will wash your clothes for you to-morrow, when it is light. Now – do not spare the water. It is cheap."

After some time Tung Lai Luk and the brigand, sitting at the Ma Jongg table in the house, were joined by Ming So and Lien Fa. The boy, lost in a pair of the girl's typically lurid pyjamas, blushed at the roar of laughter which greeted him.

" I think your laughter discourteous," he said. " My present condition is only due to my following you and finding you, my uncle, as I conceived it to be my duty to follow you. And now, having found you, I am in a house so ill-conditioned as to possess no store of spare clothes. Hence I am in debt to Lien Fa, here."

His uncle patted him on the shoulder – a rare gesture for a Chinese. " You are a good boy. Now, come and sit down. We always play a round or two in the evening, and you cannot well play worse than the man whose place you are taking. Be seated."

He stretched out his hand and began to shuffle the bamboo squares lying on the table. The house echoed with the rattle of these pieces of bamboo. Ming So shook his head suddenly, and Lien Fa wiped her eye with her handkerchief.

" I wish you would dry your hair properly," she said, as she resumed shuffling.

Chapter XXI

VIEWS OF A CRIME

" No : I have no use for men now," said The Lily. " I have had too much to do with them. All men are the same – they take what they can get from women and give nothing in return. No – I desire a quiet home in the country, where I can keep chickens and perhaps a pig or two. I have enough money saved for that."

" You are talking nonsense," said Ming So, sitting by her side on the edge of the paddy-field. A breath of wind stirred the fine blades of young rice, and the movement travelled across the field like a wave in shot silk. " You cannot live happily without men, or the gods would not have put men in the world. The gods are not wasteful. And as for you, Lien Fa, I think that you should remember what jealousy led you to do, and how nearly your crime was blamed on the innocent Yang Fei."

It was the girl's turn to be puzzled.

" Crime ? Ming So, what crime ? What crime, pray, have I committed ? "

He stared at her. " But you must be curiously constituted," he said, " not to reckon as a crime the murder of Loo Ching."

" The murder of Loo Ching ? What do you mean ? Ming, you are joking."

" I am not joking. And I think that it is very bad taste on your part to speak thus lightly of one whom you loved."

" I never loved Loo Ching," she said. " I pretended to love him – but what is this about murder ? I know nothing of it."

" You mean – I cannot believe it. You are denying it because you think that I would have nothing more to do with one whose hands were stained with the blood of a guest."

" Ming So, I swear that I do not know of what you are speaking. Listen : after Loo Ching and I had left you in your bedroom, I packed my things, or some of them, and went away. The lady Tung had said that I could go away when you two were safely locked in. Then she was to go to Loo Ching in my room. . . . Tell me what has happened."

" I will tell you what I know. But there is mystery here. I woke, to find myself alone. Yang Fei had gone. I thought, as I woke, that I had heard a cry, so I got out of bed and went to Yang Fei's room. She was not there, but on the bed lay Loo Ching, warm but quite dead."

" Men must die," said The Lily ; " but it is more pleasant for them to·die naturally. Go on."

" When I saw that Loo Ching was dead, I was silent with horror, and so I went to your room. Yang Fei was there. She said that Loo had let her out of my room while I still slept, and had taken her with him to her own room. Then, because he told her that you were asleep next door and because she knew, also, that I was asleep and did not wish to wake me, she dared not cry out. So he did what he wanted to do. Afterwards, she said, you came in and stabbed him where he lay. Then she heard you go back to your room, pack up your things, and go away. She went to your room when all was silent, not daring to lie longer with a dead man. You had gone, and she was sitting there, alone on your bed, when I came in and found her. So then I went to the room of the noble lady. She was sleeping, as was the man with her, so I telephoned, very softly, to the police, and they came and took the body away."

" Go on," said Lien Fa.

" At first they thought that it was Yang Fei who had killed him, and so I said that she had lain in my bed all the night. Then they found out that this was not true, and began to suspect me. Afterwards, when Yang Fei heard that they suspected me, she told the truth, and so you are thought to have killed Loo Ching. If you did not, who did ? "

" Surely even you can see that ? Why, the noble lady Tung, of course ! Who else ? It was always arranged that he should be thought to be with me, since then his father would not suspect."

" Why his father, Lien Fa ? "

" She desired, as I was telling my father yesterday . . . "

" Your father ? "

" Of course ! Why did you think that I was here ?

My father always affords me shelter when I come to him on holiday. Well – I was telling him that Tung and his wife desired to mortgage the business, because they could not sell it, with the Government intending to close all the houses. So she made friends with Loo Heng, who is a director of her bank, and the idea was to make the bank lend her the ten thousand dollars to ransom Tung. My father was to get a thousand for his part in the affair. With the remaining nine thousand, the two of them intended to go to Hong Kong, where the British Government allows houses such as ours, and there to start business again."

" But why did she kill the son, Loo Ching ? Surely that would not assist her plan ? " insisted the boy.

" She was jealous of this girl Yang Fei, whom she so suddenly found had taken her lover from her. Not that it seems to have been Yang Fei's intention to do so. But, you see, he went from her, leaving her asleep, and found the Yang girl. I had gone by then, of course. The lady Tung woke, found him gone, and snatched up my knife in one of her not infrequent passions."

" This is all nonsense, Lien Fa. You are inventing it for me, to try to make me believe that you did not kill Loo Ching. For how could she go to spend the night with Loo Ching, as you suggest, when all the time his father, Loo Heng, was in her own room ? Besides, both she and Loo Heng were there, asleep, when I went to telephone for the police."

The girl rose to her feet. " Let us go back to the house, if you do not believe me," she said. " But you should know that she always gave Loo Heng a sleeping-medicine in his rice when Loo Ching, the son whom she loved, was coming to the house, and you should also know that, through a closed door, it is impossible to tell if footsteps go to right or left along the passage. When Yang Fei, sitting distraught on her bed like the little fool she is, thought that she heard me moving about, she really heard Tung's wife return to her own bedroom, where she pretended to be asleep when you came, conveniently, to provide evidence that, since she was sleeping with the father, she could not have killed the son. But you do not believe me, and so it does not matter. Let us return into the house."

" It is difficult to believe, but I think that I do believe you," said the boy. " I cannot do otherwise, for I do not think it possible for women to simulate such surprise as you did when I told you of the murder of Loo Ching." Then he enquired with solicitude : " Did you love him, or was it just business ? "

But Lien Fa made no reply to this as they walked back together. When they reached the house, she said : " You will see that what I have said is true, when she comes, in three days, to pay my father the money. Then you will believe."

" In the excitement of your story, I had forgotten that surprising relationship," replied Ming So.

" Am I supposed to know that the brigand is your father ? "

" He is not a brigand now," she answered. " Lien Wo is a man of peace. But I think that you had better know nothing about it until he tells you. That would be the wiser course."

" I will be ignorant," he said. " It is always better to have a secret with a girl – life thus is more exciting."

She laughed, and went with him into the house.

Chapter XXII

SCENA

PAI MEI knelt, very much alone, before the great image of Buddha. The only human figure in that vast room, she seemed to typify the futility of man in the face of the eternal gods. But, in actual fact, little Pai Mei was conscious, at the back of her praying mind, of a strange and irrepressible doubt which assailed her. Was it really of any avail, this mewing one's sorrows, like a cat with earache, in the conjectured hearing of an image? Did Buddha really hear – did Buddha take the slightest interest in her little affairs?

Then orthodoxy descended like a pitiless heel on the small insect of her doubt, and Pai Mei prayed the more fervently because she did not quite believe.

Outside, the sun was shining.

Chapter XXIII

THE BLACK BOX

" Yes, it is true that I am afflicted with nervousness," said Loo Heng, his hand tapping insistently on the arm of his blackwood chair. " And your presence here does not in any way help to allay that nervousness, my dear Tung Nan Tsz. That you, at a time like this, should set all tongues wagging by coming here to see me in my own house, is in the highest degree unwise." He looked round him at the walls of the noble room in which they sat, his eye dwelling for an instant in turn on each of the magnificent examples of the ivory-carver's art, the skill of the worker in brass, in blackwood. . . . " It has taken me a long while and much stifling of conscience to accumulate these things," he mused, as if to himself.

Tung's wife smiled as she inspected with satisfaction the almond-shaped nails on her lap before her. At a time like this men needed very delicate handling, she reflected. But her voice showed nothing of the thoughts in her mind.

" In two days now it will be over. Your troubles will cease. May I venture to ask if you have arranged the little matter with the bank of which you are a director ? "

" That is, of course, arranged," he replied. " There was difficulty. One would almost imagine

168

that some evilly disposed person had been gossiping,
that the news had spread that I have mortgaged,
also, this house and all that it contains. But eventually I succeeded. Only nine thousand dollars, though
– they would not go to the full amount of ten thousand.
I fear that news of the intention of the interfering
Government has reached the general public."

"My dear Heng! You should not speak so dis-
respectfully of the Government of which you yourself are a member," she bantered.

"Wit is all very well in its place," he returned.
"And its place is in women's bedrooms and the
salons of the literary. Let us stick to the main facts.
Here are the documents for the mortgage for you to
sign, as you may do in the regretted absence of your
husband. Poor husband, who knows so little and
trusts so much! Here, in the space provided . . .
' Tung Nan Tsz.' . . . A fine signature. Now we
will put this away. Is there other business on which
you wished to see me? Every moment with you here
in my house fills me with foreboding. It is easy for
a man to leave his house and go pleasantly astray,
but when his pleasures come to meet him, then
danger comes too."

"Must all your birds be of an unlucky colour?"
she demanded petulantly. "You see danger where
none exists. Take care then, Loo Heng, lest by
seeing danger you expose yourself to it. For the
brave are the blind, in my opinion."

He picked up a slab of jade from the table by his

side. " Wisdom is a dear commodity," he said, reading the inscription from the slab : " for to buy wisdom one must pay with wisdom." He sighed and set the tablet down. " I wish those two days had passed. I must be getting old, thus to fret my spirit with uncalled-for misgivings. I plead in excuse that I still feel the loss of my son, in circumstances of much disgrace. Fortunately the disgrace merely brushed by me, leaving no marks. My wife, and her women also, yet mourn immoderately. For, as no doubt you, a married woman, will admit, children are an expense and a trouble, and their long dependence ill consorts with so sudden an exit from life's stage as that of Loo Ching. Even now the police tell me that there is no trace of the girl Lien Fa. Would that I had my hands on her ! "

Tung's wife rose. " I must go," she said. " Put the money into bearer bonds, so that when you and I reach Hong Kong no difficulty may occur."

" I wish that you would come away now," he said, and took her hand. " After all, there is nothing more to be gained by staying in Kwei Sek. Let us go together."

" No – I will not go until I have done that which I set out to do. There are only two days left now. Be patient, and you shall have your reward." She pressed his hand and went out by the hidden entrance. Loo Heng sighed deeply and took up again his tablet of jade.

.   .   .   .

Next day, Loo Heng walked the few paces which separated his house from the river, and, just as dusk was falling, hired the first sampan whose owner accosted him, instructing the man to make for the coaster which would sail at dawn to-morrow for Hong Kong. He intended to spend the night on board, and on the morrow Tung Nan Tsz should be back from her up-river errand. He wished that she had not insisted on going to see that foolish old Tung Lai Luk had been quietly despatched. How trusting some husbands were ! That old Tung should play the part of a captive for a whole month, in the hope that he, Tung Lai Luk, was going with his wife to Hong Kong, while all the time Tung Lai Luk would be quietly sleeping the eternal sleep somewhere amongst the river reeds, and his widow, consoled by the presence of her real lover, Loo Heng, would be safely away *en route* for the only place in China where Chinese justice could not reach her ! That was, if the police ever found out, which was unlikely. The only obviously shady side of the whole affair was the mortgaging of " The Happy Heart " and of Loo Heng's own house. He was conscious, as he sat in the sampan, of a twinge of remorse at the idea of his family finding him gone and the roof sold over their heads.

But these thoughts, these half-regrets, vanished as the sampan threaded its way towards the coaster. Loo Heng took his hand from the little shiny box wherein lay all his worldly wealth, and turned to

survey the lit strip of city which he was now leaving
for ever. How many unworthy transactions had he
made there ! How many bribes had he received !
Now all that was over, and there would be, amongst
the officials of Kwei Sek, none of the old school like
himself, only the idealistic youngsters who foolishly
imagined that the business of Government could be
carried on without recourse to the methods of the old
régime. All that was over. Now a contract for the
Public Works Department would be determined by
considerations of equity. No more would a "present"
be an essential preliminary to a business deal. . . .

Loo Heng, sitting there in the sampan, felt almost
sad at thus witnessing in his own person the passing
of the glory that was graft. Above him, on the high
bows of the coaster which was his objective, a man
sat fishing, his line visible against a green strip of sky
which still remained, a single perfect black catenary
curve on the green, from the black bows of the
steamer to the placid water over which the sampan
passed. Loo Heng smiled appreciatively at the
beauty of the quiet picture, for a taste for loveliness
cannot be denied even to absconding public servants.

Then there was a sudden crash, as a huge case of
merchandise, slipping from the hands of the coolies
on the deck of the steamer, fell on the bows of the
frail sampan, ripping through them as if through
paper. Loo Heng heard the fisherman cry : " Quick
– before the sampan sinks ! " and rose to his feet as
the water poured in through the broken planking.

But when he turned to clutch his all-important box, his hand touched only the splashed and tilting deck.

" Help ! " called Loo Heng, as his feet sank with the shattered sampan. But no help came. The man who had rowed the sampan was swimming steadily towards the shore. After all, he had no reason for complaint, since he had been given a new sampan already, advance pay for his actions in tying a knot in a fishing-line, so that it was tied to the box which had lain on the deck. . . . The fisherman on the bows of the coaster had hauled up his line a little, but only a little, for the catch was a heavy one, and as Loo Heng sank for the second time a fast motor-boat swept under the bows of the coaster, carrying with it the fisherman's line and the black box firmly tied to the end of that line. "Help !" cried Loo Heng, seeing for the last time the pale violet of the sky above him, the black mass of the steamer's bows, and hearing the shouts which denoted the attention of the ship's crew – shouts which were too late to be of much interest to Loo Heng, whose last conscious thoughts were of the unpalatable nature of slightly salt river-water.

In the launch, Tung Nan Tsz, on her way up-river, opened Loo Heng's black box. When she had located the bonds, she heaved a sigh of relief. There had been the risk that the fool would carry them in his pocket. . . .

" Haste : there is much to do to-night," she said, and at her words the motor-boat quivered at full throttle, heading up-river in the dark.

Chapter XXIV

THE HONEST BRIGAND

" Time," observed Lien Fa's parent regretfully,
" speeds on with unseemly disregard for the feelings
of such of us as would have time stand still." He sat
at his ease at the opium divan.

" That is true," answered Ming So. " Yes : I have
often found what the poet calls ' a jade minute ' pass
as though it were but the flicker of a bat's wing."

" Who told you about jade minutes ? " said the
other in an amused voice. " You know both too
much and too little. For instance, did you know
that the girl Lien Fa is the daughter of me, Lien Wo ?
Did you know this ? "

Ming So dissimulated. " I might have known," he
said, " that so delightful a daughter must have had
so distinguished a father. But one does not think of
these things until, like a pheasant rising from the
grass at one's feet, they are clear for all to see."

" Your conversation is literary," replied Lien Wo.
" I admit that your conversation is literary. But,
then, you have had opportunities, mixing as you
have done with people like your uncle and your
aunt."

" I have found little to learn from my uncle,
and nothing from my aunt," answered the boy.
" Rather have I picked up such jewels of knowledge

as I possess from the gutter of opportunity. That phrase about the jade minute, for instance . . ."

" Well ? " demanded Lien Wo, as the boy seemed to hesitate.

" I forget. And then " – he hurried on – " your own conversation, elder-born, is replete with the wisdom that comes to a man with ripening years. Your youth must have been an active one."

" It was," said Lien Wo, with regret in his voice. " More active than even you, perhaps, imagine. Ah, those were the days ! Then we recked not over-much of law and order. Each man's right hand was his government, and none said him nay."

" An exciting picture," Ming So agreed. " And now you find life dull ? "

" Yes, dull, because it is not dangerous. Ai-ah, I am getting old. Discretion sets her drab foot on adventure . . ."

" A lovely phrase ! " cried the boy.

" . . . and I do not even follow, now, where opportunity leads. Look at Tung, now ! There is a man for you. Risk – risk everywhere. His wife thinks that, since she has promised me payment, I shall do her bidding. Tung Lai Luk, wily old fox, knows what she has told me to do. She will have a rude shock when she comes here."

" My aunt is coming here ? Why ? "

" She comes in the hope, little one, of being a widow. Ah, it is so easy to arrange – an accident, a slip in the reeds on the bank of the river – but I have

not the heart to do it. The virtue is gone out of me.
I am an old man."

Ming So got up.

"It is gratifying to me to hear that my uncle's life is
safe, even if the reason for that safety is not flattering
to you. I have long wondered why my uncle was
staying here alone in this house. At first I feared for
him – then, when I realised the nature of his host, my
fears departed. But, Lien Wo, apart altogether from
this matter of your changing your mind at the dic-
tates of your better feelings, there is another sad
business nearing us. You are not aware of the
happenings at ' The Happy Heart ' ? "

" I know nothing save what my daughter tells me,
and that is only what she desires me to know,"
complained Lien Wo. " Tell me more."

" It is matter of police, I fear. You see, when Loo
Ching was murdered, it was thought to be your
daughter who killed him."

For a moment parental pride shone in the eyes of
Lien Wo. Then he said : " But that is absurd. Lien
Fa would not harm a beetle. She is kind, always.
You know how kind she is."

" I do," assented Ming So, thinking of himself and
Yang Fei, shivering and blushing at the same time
while The Lily and her lover looked on. " As you
say, she would not harm a beetle. Yet the police
think it was she who killed Loo Ching, stabbing him
in the back as he lay in the bed of Yang Fei."

" What you say is interesting, but it does not

closely concern me. My daughter, whom I sold for no inconsiderable sum to Tung Lai Luk a number of years ago now, can quite safely be trusted to look after her own interests. Yes, she brought a good price. But, then, she is undoubtedly a beauty. Do you not think so? Still " – he hesitated – " what you tell me merely confirms me in my intention not to attempt to earn the money which Tung's heartless wife promises me."

" What is it, O earner of money in strange ways, that she desires you to do ? "

" Of that, little boy, I shall not speak openly, for evil does not exist until it is done or spoken of. No : be content that your news of the murder has confirmed me in the course of virtue to which my natural tendencies would probably have led me in any event."

The boy pressed him no further, but when chance offered later he took Tung Lai Luk for a walk amongst the paddy-fields, where a man may be quite sure that conversation is heard only by those for whom it is designed.

" Lien Wo has been promised money by your honourable wife if he kills you," said the boy.

" I was not unaware of that possibility. Lien Wo and I are very good friends, although my wife fortunately does not know this. In fact . . ." He paused, as if changing the subject. " You have considerable ability in worming out information from those with whom you talk. Notice the blades

Mw

of rice in these fields at which we are looking. Notice the pale green, the perfection of tint, melting on the half-horizon to the hills and thence to the infinite sky. Consider these blades of rice, and reflect that you, Ming So, desire to make two blades of scandal spring where but one grew before. Do not, then, be so anxious to perform your verbal agri- culture, my nephew, if you wish men to attach to your words the importance which you yourself hold to be their due."

" I am sorry, my uncle, that you should think this of me, but I was so horrified when I heard of her projects. . . . How was I to know this of your honourable wife ? Is such a state of affairs to be expected ? "

Tung Lai Luk laughed. " Nonsense, little one. Do not try to make me believe that you are as inno- cent as that. Now, run along, and remember never to think either the worst or the best of a man or a woman until you have some sure basis for that judg- ment of them."

Ming So sniffed. He disbelieved in secret diplomacy.

And Tung Lai Luk, not for the first time in his life, marvelled at the ways of women. Who would have thought that his wife, when he agreed to the kidnapping idea as a convenient means of extracting money from his friends, would have added to his plan this plan of her own, the plan of having him quietly killed ? Killed, mark you, so that she might retain the ransom money ! Really, these women ! He would have to be careful, for Lien Wo was always capable of changing his mind where his pocket was concerned. . . .

Tung Lai Luk reflected that he was not at all to blame over this matter. The onus lay on the new Government of China, whose expected policy of suppressing such houses as " The Happy Heart " had made it so difficult to raise money on them in ordinary, legitimate ways. Yes, the Government was to blame.

Tung Lai Luk heaved a sigh of righteous indignation at his wife and his Government, and prepared to act accordingly.

Chapter XXV

PO FENG HSI LOSES HIS TEMPER

THE Chief of Police sat in his office. Before him lay a letter couched in unusually flowery language – a short letter, nevertheless.

" *To the honourable lady Tung*," it read.

" All preparations have been made by the unworthy writer of this letter for the reception of your noble self on the date appointed. The matter which you have entrusted to him will be despatched before your eagerly awaited coming. He has not completed the business hitherto, because not all tastes are alike in the determination of the length of time during which a pigeon should hang in summer. But the pigeon struts in the fowl-yard, ignorant of its impending fate.

" The writer trusts that his inadequate deeds will not meet with too great condemnation from the honourable lady Tung.

" LIEN WO."

Po Feng Hsi sighed. A constable tapped on the door and indicated a caller. The Chief of Police sighed again and nodded permission. Shortly the little sewing-maid from " The Happy Heart " stood before him.

"It is very dangerous for me to come here," she said ; " but the girl Yang Fei has always treated me with kindness, and so I dared the beating which the noble lady Tung will undoubtedly give me on my return."

Smiling at the child, " Go on ; tell me," he said.

" Well, this afternoon my mistress broke in the door of Yang Fei's room and, seeing me in the passage, told me to run away. After a little while, when I was downstairs, two men descended to the street, bearing the coffin of the honourable Tung Lai Luk, which, as is the custom, he keeps in the house in preparation for the day when he will *travel to the West*. They carried this coffin away, and the porter said that they were taking it to the river, to a boat. I did not think much of this at the time, because I was just going to eat my rice, but afterwards I went upstairs, and Yang Fei's room was empty. Nowhere can I find Yang Fei, who was kind to me, and I fear that my mistress has killed her and taken her away in Tung's coffin."

" But why should she do that ? " asked Po Feng Hsi, getting to his feet. " We must see at once. You return, now, as fast as your legs will bear you, to ' The Happy Heart.' We shall be there nearly as soon. Run ! " He sounded the gong on his table.

. . . .

Some rumour of impending police activity seemed to have preceded the Chief of Police, for in the narrow thoroughfare of Frog's Lane a crowd had already started to collect. Po Feng Hsi impatiently pushed his way past the porter of " The Happy Heart " ; a posse of four police followed. The porter, to whom excitements such as this constituted a welcome break in the day's monotony, sat with open mouth. Another policeman, outside the brass bars, affixed a notice, and behind him a jostling crowd craned over his shoulders to see what was written thereon. They read :

CLOSED BY ORDER OF THE POLICE.

Upstairs, Po Feng Hsi hastened from room to room, cursing silently (since he was on duty) at his foolishness in leaving the girl Yang Fei exposed to possible dangers after the accomplishment of the task which he had set her. Soon a stream of girls and women, carrying bundles of prized possessions, descended the stairs and gathered in the entrance-hall, shepherded by grinning constables whose purses, so far, had seldom allowed them access to these hidden and expensive delights.

Po Feng Hsi descended the stairs. Nearing the foot, he called for silence.

" Where is the mistress of this house, and where is the girl Yang Fei ? " he demanded of the assembled girls, and immediately a babble of information arose. When he had satisfied himself that there was no later news than that which he had already heard from the little girl, he proclaimed : " This house is closed henceforth for its accepted purpose. Pending

the return of its owners, it will be managed by
the police as a hostel for girl workers of the Government silk factory. Those of you who wish to work
in the factory will apply to the constable on duty at
the door, who will give you authority to go there.
Those who do not wish to work in the factory must
be out of here in half an hour. Permission to use the
telephone will be given for that half hour." For he
knew that many of these girls would be telephoning
to their lovers the glad news that their freedom now
needed no capital payment. . . .

As the Chief of Police stepped down to the foot of
the stairs the porter came up to him.

" And I ? " he demanded. " Is it a just thing
that a man's employment should be taken from him
thus suddenly, through no fault of his own ? If you
offer employment to these girls, you must offer it to
me, who am much more responsible."

Some of the nearest girls laughed, knowing
exactly how responsible the porter was. Po Feng
Hsi pushed the porter impatiently aside and went
out to his ricksha. A hurried call on the police
telephone might yet catch the launch. He wished
that Kung's literary advice were available.

After the usual delay, he heard the voice of the
inspector up-river. " No," said the voice ; " I
cannot stop the launch, for it passed us over an hour
ago, proceeding up-river much faster than any of
the police launches can go. Shall I telephone to the
next station ? "

" Yes. Hold the launch and all on board under arrest, and open any coffins on board," barked Po Feng Hsi. He heard the inspector's gasp of astonishment as he put back the receiver. " Order the fastest launch we have," he cried to the station chief.

" Unfortunately," replied that official, " I have to report that our fastest boat has been stolen, and would appear to be the very one which proceeded up-river last night."

At this stage the Chief of Police became horribly unintelligible.

Chapter XXVI

THE MOUSE-TRAP AND THE TIGER

To-night the moon, a flame-yellow bubble, hung just over the low bank of clouds in the west. It seemed as if the great circle of colour were about to form a drop at its lower edge, to pour a drop slowly into the darkness of the cloud-bank. The fields across the river were flooded with moonlight, but seemed in darkness, so intense was the glare of the moon : nearer, a rippling, widening cone of gold ran flickering from the shadow of the further bank to lose itself under the rushes which climbed almost to the feet of the group now seated about a small fire on the rank grass of the river edge. A faint wind disturbed the flames of the fire, and effaced, for a moment only, the outlines of the pathway of light on the water. Behind, the trees began, and behind these again stood, invisible from the river, the house of Lien Wo.

" It is a pleasant night," said Tung Lai Luk, reclining on one elbow.

" True." Lien Wo laughed softly. " Since I abandoned a life of crime – for which you, Tung Lai Luk, should be thankful – I have learned to appreciate the beauties of nature."

" It is indeed a *jade moment*," volunteered the boy Ming So, though he had not been addressed, in what was fast becoming his favourite phrase. " The moon . . ."

" There is a rabbit in the moon," said the fourth member of the group, the girl Lien Fa, in the familiar opening words of a fairy-tale which is told to very small children.

" You are a foolish woman," retorted the boy, holding her hand as he sat by her side in the firelight. " And you have forgotten again, to-day, to wash my own clothes, so that I sit here beside you looking very like a girl myself. You are foolish, for anyone but a foolish woman would begin to compose a poem about the moon, instead of telling a silly fairy-story, fit only for children. If Yang Fei were here, she would put you to shame, for she would recite a poem about the moon, even if she could not write one."

A figure advanced towards the group from the direction of the house.

" If I may be so discourteous as to intrude my unworthy person into your gathering . . ." he began, when Ming So shouted in his joy.

" Elder-born ! If it is not Kung Hiao Ling, the literary man. Why, that is exactly what we needed. A poem about the moon . . ."

" Be silent, frog ! " smiled Kung. " I am here," he went on, " as a representative of justice – a rôle which fits me as ill as this boy's clothes appear to fit him." For Ming So, in the pyjamas of the girl Lien Fa, partook a little noticeably of the grotesque.

" It is on this night, is it not, that the arrival of the evil woman Tung Nan Tsz is expected ? I should wish to be here in order to receive her."

Lien Wo, secretly, was glad of his present innocence.

" You are very welcome," he said. " After your walk – I presume that you walked – you must be suffering from that pleasant fatigue which fits perfectly with a cup of wine. Will you have one before you proceed with your story ? "

" I never refuse wine," said Kung ; " a matter of some slight expense to my politer friends. Ah, this is a good vintage ! Yes : I knew that I should find you if I followed the boy, and fortune favoured that, for when I reached the village of Nam Pa everyone was speaking of him. It appeared that, as he passed through the countryside, there passed with him a strange and unmistakable odour – the smell of dried fish. So I listened to what they had to say and followed their directions. Thus I came to your house without difficulty. Then, not desiring to trouble you with my presence until the evening of the day when the ransom for Tung Lai Luk was due to be paid, I returned to the village, where I have quietly passed my time in the enjoyment of the local wine – a vintage which was new to me. And now I fear that we have no time for further questions, for I seem to hear your sentry giving us warning of the approach of someone whom he expects."

Up the bank ran a man towards Lien Wo.

" A boat approaches, with such a roar of sound as made me think that the seven devils were in the boat."

" Heap up the signal-fire ! " ordered Lien Wo. " Tung, assume your place and strive to play the part of a dead man. The rest of you – into the nearest bushes, and listen."

" I look for entertainment which will be more than payment for my walk," said Kung Hiao Ling as he departed for the shelter of the bushes, making sure that he was within easy revolver range of the rest, for he was not minded to leave anything to chance.

The roar of the motor-boat ceased, and the glare of the powerful headlight cut across and dimmed the ladder of the moon on the river. Tung Lai Luk had dragged a coffin out of the shadow beyond the circle of firelight, and now lay down in it. Lien Wo stood beside the fire, waiting. In the bushes Ming So and Lien Fa held hands, like children at the theatre.

Then up the bank staggered two men with a burden, which they laid by the fire. Tung Nan Tsz walked beside them.

" Greetings, Lien Wo ! " she said. " I see that we have two coffins here. A fortunate precaution, was it not, for me to bring that of my husband ? It is the only wifely duty towards him which I feel inclined to perform. Now, as to its occupant. Have you done that which you promised ? Open the second coffin which you have here, and show me."

Lien Wo lifted the lid. Within lay Tung Lai Luk, his hands folded in an attitude which suggested that he had died peacefully. " My fee, noble lady," said Lien Wo, who did not easily forget little matters like this. He wished that he were not quite so alone – the two men whom she had brought with her stood beside the woman, and he had not reckoned on this. So he directed their attention to the coffin which had been carried up from the launch. " Open it," he said, and the men moved forward to obey.

" There is a further present for you, there in that coffin," said Tung Nan Tsz. " I had no further use for the girl, and she had angered me, so I brought her for you to use as you thought best. Here is your reward, in money " – she handed Lien Wo a wad of notes – " and there in flesh."

For the coffin-lid had been removed, revealing Yang Fei, trussed hand and foot, and gagged.

" But this is a very handsome present," said Lien Wo, as he bent over the girl in the coffin. He hoped that, while the attention of Tung Nan Tsz and her men was thus directed, an attack might be made from the rear. So he continued his praise of Yang Fei, lying there in the coffin with only her eyes moving. " I am honoured by your forethought, for while a payment in cash is pleasant, how much more pleasant is payment in the body of a young girl like this. I am, it is true, past middle age, but, even so, I feel now emotions which have long lain hidden."

Why did not the woman reply, or Kung lead on the attack? Then, sounding hollowly from the other coffin, he heard an unmistakable sneeze. On the sound, Tung's wife cried to her men.

" To the boat! It is a trap! Run!" she called.

Lien Wo turned. In the flickering light of the fire he could see Tung Lai Luk, sitting foolishly upright in his coffin. From the river bank came the sound of flying feet, and with a roar the engine of the motor-boat broke into life.

" They have escaped you!" cried Tung Lai Luk. " Why did you not stop the evil woman?"

" I could not," answered Lien Wo. "Did you not see that she had with her two men, and that both she and her men were armed? Do I desire to *go finally to the West* before I have reached a ripe old age? What could I do? I occupied her with conversation, hoping that the others would attack while I held her attention. Fancy choosing such a moment to sneeze! The fault is yours. All would have been well if you had not sneezed."

" How can a man forgo sneezing when a woman scatters pepper over him?" Tung Lai Luk complained. " She scattered it over my face as if I were a piece of meat to be rendered appetising. I suppose she wished to see if I were really dead. How little trustful are women!"

Kung Hiao Ling emerged from the darkness beyond the light of the fire.

" It is fortunate," he observed, " that she did not

He tore at
the fastening
of her gag

think of making the test as to your being alive by the simple expedient of making sure with a dagger or a revolver bullet. It seems to me that a nose full of pepper is better than a belly full of steel or lead. You are lucky, Tung Lai Luk. She is a more evil woman that I had expected. I could not fire because, in this darkness, I could not be sure who was friend, who foe. And Ming So, who at any rate was not lacking in courage, whatever one may say of his discretion, was pushed off the back of the motor-boat by the woman. Here he is now."

The boy Ming So presented an unattractive figure, for he had fallen into the mud which bordered the river, and his borrowed garments were now no longer gaudy. He had fallen over backwards from the departing stern of the motor-boat, and half his face, too, was muddy. But, despite this, he was the first to remember Yang Fei, lying there bound and gagged in the coffin.

" Hurry," cried the boy. " Have you no belly of compassion, that you let her remain in a coffin as if she were dead ? " For to him Yang Fei meant just a little more than to the rest. He remembered the " Ballad of Everlasting Wrong," and the night in Kwei Sek when he had gone to sleep naked on her lap in the locked room. . . . He tore at the fastenings of her gag, and the others came to help him.

.   .   .   .

When Yang Fei had been released from her bonds and was restoring the circulation in her limbs in front of the fire, Lien Wo came over, rubbing his hands.

"The girl is not damaged?" he enquired.

Tung Lai Luk turned on him in a fury. "You, muddler and bungler!" he cried. "You! Interested in the possible damage to her, as if she were a roll of silk, to be bandied about from owner to owner! I would have you know that I bought this girl for good money, as my nephew here can bear witness, that I bought her for good money from her father, who lives in the village of Seung So, and that she belongs to me."

Kung Hiao Ling said, quietly: "Under the constitution of the Republic it is illegal to buy and sell girls. I think that you, Tung Lai Luk, and you, Lien Wo, might be better occupied than in your present wrangle about a girl who belongs to neither of you, but to herself. So let us have no more of this. There are more serious matters which concern us, for I ought to return to the village and communicate to the Chief of Police what has happened. But, since I know that the woman will expect me to do so, (since it is the obvious thing to do), I shall not return. It does not do to act as is expected. Therefore I shall listen to the tale which the girl has to tell. Give her a cup of wine, to warm her blood. I, also, could drink without discomfort, for it is late. Already the dawn makes feeble efforts to overcome the glory of the moon."

"It is not fair," objected Lien Wo. "She was

given to me, as was this money, my payment for killing the woman's husband. I begin to wish, Tung Lai Luk, that I had not been so squeamish."

Kung held out a hand for the notes, glanced at them, fingered one. "Forgeries," he said, handing them back. "She was indeed a very evil woman. Now " – and he completely ignored the curses of the ex-bandit – " tell me your story, girl, and omit nothing."

Yang Fei trembled a little at the prospect of so large and unusual an audience. "I was put in a coffin," she began hesitatingly, " and the lid was put on, but not tightly." She began to warm up to her tale. "Then I was carried to a boat, and after a while I heard the motor begin. I lay in the coffin, unable to move. Then there was, after a time, a shout, and the sound of a box moving on the deck, and I heard her voice."

"What did she say ? " asked Kung.

"She said : ' Now that he is drowned and I have the money, there is little else to do. Haste,' the woman called, ' for we must speed up-river, where a husband awaits me.' That is all she said. After a long time, the boat stopped and I was carried up here. The rest you know." She emptied her wine-cup. "And now may I go to rest, for I am tired, and my limbs hurt where the cord cut into them. . . ."

Kung Hiao Ling led the way back to the house and issued orders as if he were in his own rooms above the wine-shop in Kwei Sek. But nobody

Nw

seemed to think of disobeying him. Even Lien Wo, cursing still at the trick of the forged notes, did not protest when Yang Fei was put to bed and left with Lien Fa to watch by her side. Kung assembled them in the largest room of the house. Outside, the dawn crept up as if pursuing the moon, where it had sunk below the horizon opposite.

" We must take counsel together," he said, " though I fear that counsel is useless at the moment. But I wish to collect the facts on paper so that I may lay them before Po Feng Hsi, the Chief of Police, on my return to the city, or may perhaps send them to him by police messenger. There are, in this matter, more mysteries than one."

Ming So, who returned from washing at this moment, yawned. Old Kung was apt to be prosy, he felt. Here was the hour of the ascent of the morning, and Kung must go and collect evidence. Further, the new pair of Lien Fa's pyjamas (a flaming red this time) fitted even less well than the last pair had done.

Chapter XXVII

THE ODYSSEY OF AN OPTIMIST

THE little girl Pai Mei, squatting on her heels in the lean-to kitchen, rocked gently back and forth like a a small automatic figure. At intervals the rhythm of her rocking was interrupted by a sob which shook her small body ; then she would return again to the endless slicing of beans from the bowl on the mud floor in front of her.

Outside, a gentle wind disturbed the bamboos in the thicket, so that they rustled in the distance almost as silk rustles. The pale moon above the bamboos sent not enough light to show through the paper window against the greater light of the hanging oil lamp in the kitchen, but Pai Mei knew that the moon hung there, for she had just opened the door and glanced out, shutting the door again hurriedly as Ming Nai's querulous voice came to her from the living-room.

" Must you for ever be opening the door to let in the cold ? " The voice demanded this without eliciting a reply, and Pai Mei had quickly returned to the slicing of her beans, while in her mind's mirror the narrow sickle of cream-silver topped the tracery of the bamboos as it used to do when she and Ming So went into the clump of an evening.

How many moons had passed since their parting ?

How many moons and how few letters? He seemed to have so much else to do, so many other interests than the little girl who now squatted on her heels, sorrowfully slicing beans for her mistress. The gods in their pale palaces of amber cloud above her alone knew what Ming So would be doing now, she thought. Doubtless he had found some other girl, and forgotten his promises to Pai Mei. Men were faithless creatures, blown by every wind of fancy from girl to foolish girl, constant never, trading affection against a moment's delight, following their inclinations rather than clinging with a woman's constancy to one beloved.

A tear ran down one cheek and fell into the beans. She brushed off the next tear and laid down the knife. This was a turning-point, she felt. Had not the boy told her that, if Ming Nai became unbearable, Pai Mei was to take the money for the journey from the medicine-chest and go to join him in the city? That was the only way. She would wait until Ming Nai was asleep, and then take the money and go. How much money? She did not know, but it would be as well to take most of it, for you never knew how much expense there would be. And, after all, the money was doing nothing there in the drawer of the medicine chest, not even earning interest. . . .

Pai Mei's fingers flickered as she sliced beans, now that her mind was made up.

.   .   .   .

At the " hour of the rat " the moon now floated clear, high in the purple-black velvet night. Everywhere stars were dusted on this sky, carelessly, irregularly, as gems fall from the hand of a miser and glow patiently in the lamplight. Just below the moon a single inexplicable cloud hung, the only soft outline in all that cardboard sky. The wind had dropped, and the tops of the tall trees bordering the road to Ch'ang Sui climbed to the fringe of the forest and seemed to have been frozen there, in the last moment of their mad aspiring for a marriage of tree and sky. The brilliance of the moon gave to the greenery a semblance of partly seen whiteness, so that the small blue-clad figure of Pai Mei, her thick paper soles silent on the dried mud of the road, might have been moving in the vast drop-scene of some empty theatre as she steadily plodded along the path towards the river. In an inner pocket lay nearly all the money which Ming Nai had saved against a possible bad winter.

As she walked, Pai Mei sang softly to herself the " Ballad of Mulan," to keep her company between the towering, clutching trees. Mulan had been just such another girl as she, Pai Mei thought. Only Mulan had gone to the wars to take the place of her father. She would like to go as a soldier, too, marching, marching, as she was now across interminable distances, in the Emperor's service. But there wasn't any Emperor now – only a Republic, whatever that meant. . . . Then she could come back from

the wars, and everyone would be surprised to find
she was a girl.   How did it finish ?

> *" For the man hare gallops awkwardly*
> *And the woman hare's eye is wild,*
> *But if they are running together,*
> *Who can tell which is which ? "*

She came to the end of the song, and in the
motionless silence between the great trees the
shuffle of her feet sounded like the movement of an
army. . . .

.   .   .   .

Ch'ang Sui was easy to negotiate.   Arriving even
before dawn, Pai Mei had leisure to look round and
make a few enquiries in an apparently casual
manner.   It appeared, as the result of these enquiries,
that a passenger boat left at dawn for the next
village, Seung So, whence, perhaps, she might be
able to obtain another boat down-river.

On board, she paid her passage-money and ate
a stomachful of the dried *lichees* which she had
bought in Ch'ang Sui.   *Lichees* were a luxury to
which she was unaccustomed, and she felt that it
would be foolish, with so much money at her
disposal, to deny herself the pleasure of eating them.
Then she lay down amidst a pile of rope in the bows
and fell fast asleep. . . .

She woke several hours later.   In fact, the sinking
sun told her that the village of Seung So must be

not very far off. She sat up amidst her coil of rope
and yawned. So far, so good. This travelling was
an easy matter if you only had the intelligence and
the necessary money. The money – her hand went
to her jacket pocket, to find it empty.

.   .   .   .

The two parents sat facing each other in Pai
Kwat's private room. But it was daylight now, and
the little lamp above his head had not been lit. On a
chest against the wall lay the *I-Ching* – the Book of
Changes. In brass holders in the four corners of the
room were stuck the thin charred wooden sticks
which had last night held on their upper ends
brownish, blunted cylinders of *heung*. The room still
smelled faintly acid, for the fumes of their burning
had not completely disappeared, and on Ming Nai's
tongue, as she talked, the air tasted with a suspicion
of a bitter tang.

" So she has gone – disappeared – and I have not
the money to set on foot enquiries as to her whereabouts," concluded Ming Nai.

" What you tell me fills me with misgiving as to my
wisdom in allowing her to go to live in your house,"
replied Pai Kwat. " For if a girl runs away, two
things must have caused it : first, she has been ill-
treated ; and, second, she has not been fittingly
instructed in the paths of virtue by those to whom
she has been entrusted. Yes, I begin to think that I
was very unwise."

Ming Nai was not in the least abashed. " You have," she replied, " taken no account of two other facts, both of which colour somewhat the blackness of your picture. First, that the child ran away in order to go to my son in the city. This, you must acknowledge, shows devotion and constancy. Second, it is the first four years of a child's life which determine that child's character, and during those four years she learned, apparently, to take whatever money she happened to need from whomsoever it might belong to. This, I think, reflects adversely on your own treatment of the girl, Pai Mei."

Pai Kwat sat looking straight in front of him at a scroll on which was written in characters of singular beauty and skill in caligraphy the sentence : *Deal with the faults of others as gently as you deal with your own.* But this was too difficult to act on, when this woman sat there criticising his daughter.

" It is impossible for a roast fowl to lay eggs," he replied. " An argument cannot be applied to only one fact of several – it must be applied impartially to all. If I am to blame for my daughter's action, I am equally to be praised for other actions of hers which are good. I may be criticised for her taking the money without permission. But when you advance her devotion and constancy, as you did a moment ago, I am to be praised, on your own argument. When you talk thus, you must talk fairly. The result of all your speech is that the girl is a mixture of good and bad, even as I am, and even as you yourself are. Need we pursue that line of argument further ? "

Baffled (for she had hoped for either money or the offer of another of the numerous Pai children), Ming Nai could not but agree.

" I suppose that you are right," she said. " And, even if you were not, it is absurd to expect so learned a man to admit his error to a woman."

This touched Pai Kwat on his conscience, for there is a saying of the Master, Confucius, to the effect that *to have faults and fail to amend them, this is indeed to have faults.* And he knew that Ming Nai was referring to this saying. So he observed, very humbly : " If I have faults, I ought to admit them. If I have failed in her education, the fault, then, is mine ; I admit it. But surely you are exaggerating the escapade ? Either she will return or, as is more likely, she will safely reach Kwei Sek and her beloved affianced. In either case, the outcome will be felicitous. Why, then, repine ? *The highest towers begin from the ground,* and I have little doubt that my daughter and your son will eventually grow to be much like their parents."

Ming Nai rose. " Long visits bring short compliments," she observed. " I am woman enough to prefer longer compliments. No – do not be so formal as to ring for a parting cup of tea. I will take the will for the deed. Now that my duty is done, and I have told you the facts so far as I know them, my mind is at rest."

" Walk well, then," returned Pai Kwat, reflecting that now he would be able to begin again his study of the *I-Ching*, in which he had been interrupted by her arrival.

" Walk well, you also," said Ming Nai, as she went out, back to her empty house.

Chapter XXVIII

HOW TO MAKE A WIDOW

Yang Foo issued orders to his family.

" My wife, you will busy yourself with the evening food, as is your duty. The two boys will fetch the water-buffalo to her new pasture, driving in the stake for her rope very firmly indeed, for to-day she is restive with the spring fever of animals, and desires to leave us. The girl children will now fetch my nets, which have been mended, I hope, and bear them to the boat. There, that is all, I think. There is a sufficiency of time for a few breaths of leisure ere I start."

His aged wife stood before him, as is fitting even in the wife of a fisherman-farmer. " All shall be done as you say," she agreed. " Oh, my husband, I know that I am a foolish woman, but I cannot help repining."

He smiled. " Again ? Can you never forget the sale of your daughter, Ah Fei ? Must you for ever be throwing in my teeth the poverty which compelled us to sell the girl ? There is no bottom to the well of the foolishness of women ! We have no such daughter. Let us forget our daughter. Probably by now she is earning her rice, which is more than you are, standing there wailing ! What is done cannot be undone, and *it is useless to repine over things that are past*." He rose to his feet. " My wife, dry your tears and begin preparing the food against my return. Your late daughter, whose state so concerns you, is doubtless lying now in an honourable bed, and, after all, that is the end for which the gods created women."

She followed him to the door and called after him. " Have a care," she cried, " for the night is foggy here by the river, and a foot may slip . . ."

" To anticipate the tiger is as bad as meeting the tiger," was Yang Foo's reply as he walked off towards the river bank, where he could hear the chatter of the girls, returning after setting his nets in the little sampan. " Be comforted : even the worst has an end."

His wife wiped her eyes and went into the kitchen.

.   .   .   .

" We shall just reach Seung So," said the coxswain of the motor-boat, " if the petrol is sufficient. But I doubt whether, at that unimportant village, we shall be able to buy more petrol without causing comment. That is a matter for you to decide."

Tung Nan Tsz laughed scornfully.

" We do not desire to purchase petrol at Seung So. That would be the height of folly. No – it is only a little distance now, and we shall complete the journey in the sampan which I now see coming in this direction. Steer towards it."

The coxswain knew better than to argue with his mistress. But he sniffed audibly as he swung the wheel over and the motor-boat bore down on the little craft whose one occupant, an old man, stood in the stern sculling steadily downstream. In the bows lay a pile of fishing-nets.

The launch bumped alongside, and the second man jumped into the sampan.

" What thing ? " rose the protesting, thin voice of the old fisherman. " What thing ? You jump into my boat. . . ." His voice subsided into a wet grunt as the knife took him in the ribs. With a careless kick the man from the motor-boat thrust the body into the stream.

Tung Nan Tsz looked carefully up and down the river. For the five hundred yards before it curved towards the village there was not a soul to be seen. Downstream, likewise, was empty.

" Lift the box into the sampan," she ordered, and the two men obeyed, setting it down on the top of the nets. " Now : sink the launch, here in mid-stream." She sat watching while, with an axe, the coxswain smashed through the bottom boards and stepped into the sampan.

" You do your work badly," she said. " Look – the launch is sinking too slowly." Both men gazed at the motor-boat, and Tung Nan Tsz drew an automatic from the folds of her jacket and fired. These men constituted the last piece of direct evidence against her. She fired twice, at point-blank range, and gave the nearest man a push with her foot as he fell, so that he splashed overboard, cursing.

The coxswain coughed once and lay still. The woman took the single scull of the sampan and, using it as a lever, tilted the body into the stream. Then she removed a slight blood-stain from the deck, where the coxswain had fallen, using a piece of waste cloth from the bottom of the sampan, threw the rag into the river, and leisurely took her place at the stern, driving the little boat up-river towards the village of Seung So just round the bend.

The launch had filled and now took a sudden plunge, stern up, as the weight of the engines dragged it under water.

Alone, on the mirror surface of the water, Tung Nan Tsz sculled the sampan upstream in the gathering dusk.

By and by her muscles began to tire of the unaccustomed labour. Seung So was farther off than she had thought, and the steady current made each stroke of the scull a labour. She swung the sampan in towards the left bank, and here, in the slightly slower water, made better progress. But, even thus, Seung So remained tantalisingly round the corner, and dusk fell quietly like a grey cloak on the calm river, the silhouetted reeds, and the full purple cloud-bank.

Then, sitting on the bank level with the sampan, Tung Nan Tsz noticed a small girl squatted, head on her hands, crying.

" Ho la ! " called the woman in the boat. " Do you wish to earn money ? "

The child lifted her head as the boat drew in. "Oh, yes," she replied. "To earn money is the very thing which I desire, for I have none. I have been sitting here for hours, seeing nothing through my tears. . . ."

"Then come and aid me with this sampan," said the woman, "for I am late in returning to the village, and dusk is falling."

"I will gladly help," Pai Mei said. "But I do not think that, even so, we should reach Seung So in less than two hours, and I am weak from want of food. Would it not be wiser to tie the boat to the bank and walk to the village? I would look after the boat until your return."

The woman stepped out, holding the painter. "You have sense," she said. "But we shall leave the boat, you and I, and go to the house which I see at the far side of these paddy-fields, with a single lighted room. They are probably poor people who will gladly sell us a night's lodging."

"Then you will not require my help," said Pai Mei, "for your box appears light enough for you to carry yourself. But could I not earn the money which you promised by remaining here to look after the boat? I am not *very* hungry, and to-morrow you could pay me." Once she could get aboard the sampan, it would be easy to drift and scull down the stream, towards Ming So. . . .

"You will carry my box to the house, as I said," Tung Nan Tsz answered. "I will pay you when it is necessary. but to-night you shall eat at my expense. Come, here is the box for you to carry." She released her hold on the painter as she handed to Pai Mei the shiny black case containing the worldly wealth of the late Loo Heng.

" Ai-ah ! The boat ! " cried the girl, making an ineffectual attempt to catch the gunwale of the retreating sampan.

" No matter, we shall not need it now," replied Tung Nan Tsz. " And remember, child, that if I pay you for serving me, I pay you also for keeping a silent tongue. You know nothing, you understand, of any such boat or any such happenings. All that you know is that you met me on the bank of the river and that I engaged you as my servant. Beyond that, do not talk. Now, walk ! For I am hungry, and even the single light yonder means some sort of food. What is your name, child ? "

Pai Mei, even at her tender age, had acquired some of that worldly wisdom which comes early to those in poverty. And in her mind hovered the memory of the money which she had taken and the possible penalty if she was caught before she managed to reach the city and Ming So. She therefore replied, without a moment's hesitation, smiling : " I am an orphan. My father's name was Woo, but now he is dead, and I am going to the city of Kwei Sek, to an aunt who lives in the Street of the Dressmakers, and I had not seen anyone for hours, until you came in the boat. . . ." It was a safe reply,

for Woo is a common name, and there is a Street of
the Dressmakers in every city.

Satisfied, Tung Nan Tsz walked along beside her.
" You may call me Mistress Pak," she said, giving
another common surname, and left it at that, as the
two plodded on along the raised banks between
paddy-fields, towards the warm and comforting
glow of the lit window in the house ahead.

When they reached this house, Tung Nan Tsz
knocked, and after a shuffling and whispering an old
woman came and peered through a hole in the door.

" What business have you, when dark is falling ? "
she demanded.

" I desire shelter for the night for myself and this
small servant of mine," was the answer.   " Open
the door, for a chill rises from the river."

" I dare not give you lodging," grumbled the old
woman.   " Until he returns you may enter, and
when he returns you may ask him.   How many are
you ? "

" We are two only, I and this child," returned
Tung Nan Tsz impatiently, for she was not used to
having her wishes disregarded.   " Let us in, and we
will await his return, if you say that we must.   Who,
then, is this ' he ' ? "

The bar behind the door was lifted, the wood
swung inwards, and in the unaccustomed light Tung
Nan Tsz blinked as she stepped across the thres-
hold, followed by Pai Mei.

" He is my husband, Yang Foo, and he is now
Ow

laying his nets in the river. He will not be above an hour," answered the woman. Her lined face and toil-worn hands told of a precarious existence wrested from the soil. " Until then you may sit down in this room, and if you will pay now I will give you each a bowl of the rice which we are now about to make. That is all which I can provide at the moment, for we are poor and did not expect the honour of a visit."

Tung Nan Tsz drew money from a pocket. By no signs at all did she indicate her knowledge that the family of Yang would wait in vain for the return of Yang Foo, who was doubtless well down the river by now, quite unconscious of what went on in the house.

" There is money," she said. " Now, produce your rice, for we are both hungry, this girl and I."

Yang Foo's unwitting widow called orders, and shortly her smallest daughter emerged with two bowls of steaming rice.

" My husband has two sons and six daughters, for we were compelled to sell one to a merchant of Kwei Sek some weeks ago. This is the youngest." Even in the poorest house there is a certain pride in progeny, even in female progeny. " Come, set to and eat, and when he comes back from the river we may talk about lodging."

Then the room was silent but for the steady click of chopsticks on cheap china bowls.

.   .   .   .

The meal was over. Rice-bowls had been removed and presumably washed. Round the little brazier the family of Yang squatted, while their two guests, unheeded, sat on the only available chairs. Pai Mei would have felt much more at her ease – and much warmer – if she had joined the squatting family, but she dared not, at the present juncture, initiate an action. Her own position was not such that she could afford to take risks with this strange woman whom chance had thrown in her way when all other hope had failed and despair had crept towards her up the river bank with the first mists of evening. She must remain dutifully obedient, she must sink her own personality, until her pay had accumulated sufficiently to allow her to proceed down-river to the city of Kwei Sek in search of Ming So. Then she could tell the police, if they paid her to do so, about the sunken launch which she had seen and the revolver shots, and the three dead men in the river. . . .

Of course, her childish analysis of the position admitted no such advanced ideas as these – her reactions and thoughts were on a simpler, lower plane, though they reached the same conclusion. Thus she sat stiffly on the chair, envying the family of Yang as they squatted round their brazier.

After the time that it takes a man to plough two furrows of a paddy-field, Tung Nan Tsz spoke.

" The master of the house is late," she said, " but I and my servant are weary. Could we be shown to a room where we may sleep, for I am certain that the honourable Yang Foo, when he returns, will not refuse us shelter in his house."

The old woman by the brazier said : " He should be here now at any moment. You will await him. It is not fitting for women to take decisions."

The elder of the two sons spoke now, a strapping lad of some seventeen summers. " I think, mother, that when my father returns he will be angry with us if we compel these visitors of ours to wait thus uncomfortably for his arrival. Would he not rather wish us to provide them with a room and settle in the morning what money it is fitting for them to pay ? "

His mother nodded agreement. " Maybe you are right, and if, when my honourable husband returns, he considers that we have done wrong, I shall say that the idea was yours, my son." She rose to her feet and opened the swinging doors of the room beyond the one in which they were sitting. " Ah Yat ! Ah Sam ! " she cried, and the two eldest girls rose with her. " Remove such things as it would not be fitting to leave in this room, that our visitors may pass a comfortable night."

Pai Mei watched with relief, for, despite a bowl of rice, she was very tired, and the indefinite postponement of her plans had brought tears very near the surface. . . .

When the little oil lamp had been blown out, Pai Mei lay in her borrowed bedding listening to the regular breathing of her sleeping employer. Outside, bull-frogs kept up their bell-chorus, and once, just before she went to sleep, a gust of cold air blew in and a door slammed. Presumably the two sons were going out to look for Yang Foo. But Pai Mei did not remain awake in order to think of these problems. She laid her neck on the hard wood pillow and was soon in a dreamless sleep.

Chapter XXIX

THREE PROBLEMS

Po Feng Hsi, Chief of Police for the city of Kwei
Sek, sat now at a long table in the small police
station at Nam Pa, the village which lay one day's
journey by water up the river from the city where he
normally found more than enough crime to exercise
his mind. But this matter of the murder of Loo
Ching, the son of the Kwei Sek Minister of Public
Works, the subsequent disappearance of Loo Heng,
the Minister himself, as well as of the boy Ming So,
of Yang Fei, and her mistress Tung Nan Tsz, together with the undoubted theft of one of his own
police launches, had so far incensed Po Feng Hsi
that he had left the care of the city's crimes in the
hands of a subordinate, and was now spreading
wrath and inspiration round the little village of
Nam Pa.

" The stolen launch passed Nam Pa, but has not
reached the next day's stop, Seung So ? " he
demanded.

" That is so," assented the local officer. " What do
you deduce therefrom, O unraveller of mysteries ? "

" I deduce," said Po Feng Hsi, rising to his full
height, " that the launch is somewhere in between
the two villages." A deferential silence greeted this
wild guess, and he went on : " You have notes of the

time when the launch passed Nam Pa, going upstream, and of the time when the patch of oil,
smelling of petrol, swept past Nam Pa on its way to
the sea ? "

" We have notes of these," agreed the other.

" The stream runs, in the average, three feet a
second, and the launch was capable of a speed of
fifty *li* an hour. Now go and calculate how far the
launch must have gone upstream before she was
deliberately sunk, in order that the consequently
freed petrol should reach Nam Pa on the bosom of
the stream at the time which you have noted." He
lit a cigarette. " Now let Kung produce a more
capable piece of detective work ! " he muttered to
himself, as he went out of the police station, leaving
behind him perspiring policemen busy with clicking
abacus, writing-brush, and paper.

.   .   .   .

At Lien Wo's house, Kung Hiao Ling was sitting
pensively in the garden, watching the river. Beside
him lay a borrowed jade-studded opium pipe and a
paper-covered copy of the poems of Li Po. The boy
Ming So appeared from the house with a fresh
supply of wine.

" Has inspiration followed in the footsteps of the
grape ? " the boy asked.

For answer Kung took up the book of Li Po's
poems and read :

> " *The nightjar wails its absent mate,*
> *And Youth grows old amongst the hills.*

Ah, Li Po was a poet! I think that our actions should be dictated less by a desire to apprehend the evil woman Tung than by a desire to set right some of the evil which she has brought about."

" You refer, O wise sir, to what ? "

" I refer, Ming So, to your little friend Yang Fei, who has suffered much, and must desire to return, at any rate for a time, to her father's house. If I do not misunderstand the child – and indeed her knowledge of geography is not great – she lives near Seung So, which is one day's journey up the river. I propose to take her there."

" But, master, the evil woman Tung . . . "

" The evil woman Tung also proceeded up-river. To eat two dishes with one spoon amuses me at times. Will you come ? "

" I will come wherever you go, Master, for I have never before met one who so satisfactorily combines duty with delight, who so excellently reads in the poets instructions for action. I will come with you, if you will let me."

" Ask the remainder, then, what they feel, and if enough of them are agreed on the need for a voyage up-river, we will hire men and a boat from this village of Nam Pa. Go now, for I wish to read."

Ming So bowed profoundly and withdrew as Kung stretched out his hand for the wine-jar.

.   .   .   .

In the daylight Pai Mei realised how extremely sordid were the surroundings of the house where they had found refuge and shelter. The three rooms which she had seen were bare of every comfort and convenience save those fundamental necessities which served to feed the family and to protect them from the weather. Outside the house the remains of a shed contained a primitive plough and a few ancient agricultural instruments : on the edge of a near-by field the water-buffalo grazed, her black head bent to the scanty pasture available. A discarded fishing-net hung along some stunted bushes on the eastern side of the buildings.

"But how," she asked of the youngest Yang daughter, "do your family continue to live ? For here I do not see a sufficiency of either food or implements to support so many mouths."

"We live on the fish which my honourable father catches from the river," replied the child. "And, now that my father has not returned, we shall starve except for such rice as we have stored and such money as your mistress pays us."

"That is an evil state of affairs," observed Pai Mei, her little head on one side, for she had never sampled quite such abject poverty as this. "You say that your father has not returned ? Did not your brothers find him last night, then ? "

"No. They found his boat, with his nets in, caught in a backwater, two *li* downstream. But of my father there was no sign. Tell me, from what direction did you and your mistress come last night ? "

" I was sitting on the river bank as dusk was falling," said Pai Mei, as she had been instructed. " The woman came up to me and asked me if I would carry her black box, and I agreed, for I was hungry and I had no money. That is all I know."

" It is strange that she should have been on the bank," objected the younger child. " For no man walks by the river, save such as do not know the country, or those who have to cultivate it, since the road runs far away, by those trees yonder." She pointed to the horizon. " And you, too, why were you on the river bank ? "

" Because I had walked there," Pai Mei replied. " Come ; we must go in, for there are, doubtless, duties which my mistress has invented for me." She turned and re-entered the house.

By and by the old woman came into the room where Tung Nan Tsz sat on her black box.

" You were on the river bank last night," she said. " My honourable husband was also on the river bank, and he has not returned, as you know. Did you not see him ? "

Tung Nan Tsz assumed a magnificent disregard. " Last night ? I do not remember seeing any man last night," she said. " And I am becoming hungry. When will the morning rice be cooked ? "

" There is no rice here until you tell me all you know," said the old woman. " Where did you see Yang Foo on the river bank, and what was he doing when you saw him ? "

" I tell you, I do not remember seeing any man – only this small girl, whom I engaged as my servant. And if you do not soon produce the morning rice, I shall be compelled to take myself, my servant, and my payment elsewhere, to a house where more attention is paid to the requirements of guests who are prepared to pay for them."

The old woman went out grumbling, and by and by her voice called Pai Mei to come and fetch the two rice-bowls for the morning meal.

No more was said, and the day passed without any happening until again dusk rubbed out the clear lines of the paddy-fields and the lamp was lit. Pai Mei felt an absurd sense of impending danger, she knew not why. The two sons moved sullenly about the house on duties which did not exist, and the girls crouched over the brazier.

" We shall move on to-morrow," said Tung Nan Tsz. " I find that the food here is not as good as life in a city has led me to expect."

" In the city ? You live in the city of Kwei Sek ? Then you will know of Ming So, who . . . "

" Silence, talkative one ! Do you wish all the world to know ? "

But the world had a very good idea now, and Pai Mei's treble question had spurred others to action. The two sons appeared in the doorway : the old woman Yang stood behind them.

" What is in that black box ? " one of the sons demanded, advancing into the room.

" And, in reply, what is that to do with you ? "
demanded Tung Nan Tsz. But the family of Yang
took no notice of this : they suspected her, and they
were determined to settle for themselves the problem
of the contents of the box and the business, if any,
which had brought this masterful woman to their
house at the moment when, by an incredible
coincidence, their father had disappeared into the
thin air of the river banks.

Pai Mei sat in a corner.

" Don't you run away ! " commanded the old
woman.

" And why should I desire to run away ? " asked
Pai Mei in return. " I have not yet received my
pay from my mistress, and therefore to run away
is the last thing in my mind."

Nevertheless two of the Yang girls were detailed
to look after Pai Mei while the rest of the family
pursued their investigations. . . .

Chapter XXX

DOVES OF EXPERIENCE

Tung Lai Luk stretched out his arms lazily on each side of the wicker chair in which he lay at length, and yawned prodigiously.

" Praise be to the eternal gods," he said, " that now we have, for a brief enough space, to endure none of our late trials – the energy of Po Feng Hsi, the epigrams of Kung Hiao Ling, the shrill piping of the boy, my nephew Ming So, nor the moonlike face of his little friend Yang Fei. Quite apart from my regrettable wife's efforts to rid herself of me." He yawned again, for it was pleasantly hot here in the garden of Lien Wo's house near Nam Pa. Then he suddenly remembered this Lien Wo in his catalogue. " Or, for that matter, the spurious but worldly wisdom of your excellent father," he concluded.

Lien Fa, with a swift stroke of her fan, ended the scavenging career of a fly in the neighbourhood of Tung Lai Luk.

"That is all very true," she agreed. "Here in the silent garden one may assemble unhurried thoughts."

He looked round, surprised. " Are you, also, an epigrammatist ? " he demanded.

The girl nodded her head, as the Chinese do when they wish to express denial. " No," she answered.

" I do not aspire to be literary. No. I only know that life is pleasant here, with you in the chair before me and no duties nor distractions to torment me. I could spend many hours like this, defending you from the assaults of flies. Further, I could spend these hours with pleasure."

He laughed. " Because I am old and fat, you are pleased to be facetious. Really, you desire to be off, back to the places where life is gay and brightly coloured, where young impulse and its gratification are not separated by the abyss of middle-aged inertia."

" You wrong me as much as you wrong yourself," she replied. " I have had enough of the delights of youth, as you call them. Some pastimes are over-rated, and that is one of them. No : I desire now the comparative peace such as that which we are now enjoying – if I may venture to say so – are enjoying together."

He turned to look at her. Then, apparently satisfied, he said : " You may venture to say so, for there is in your words more than a grain of truth. I, too, have lately been thinking how delight-ful it would be to put behind us this medley of intrigue and duty, and to begin again in some other place to taste what life has so far denied us."

" But," she contended, moving the fan slowly, "what has life denied us ? You have money, property, and a wife. What more may a man desire ? "

"A man may desire much more than money, property, and a wife, Ah Fa." And, as he addressed her thus informally, she smiled behind the moving fan. "We may desire sons, for instance. My wife has, unfortunately, been unable to supply them. Or even daughters. And then a man needs a wife in something more than name only. My excellent if lawless wife serves but as a peg whereon to hang the personal adornments which my money serves to purchase. No – it is not enough."

The girl made no reply. She knew that, before long, he would continue. And in this she was right, for Tung Lai Luk turned half round in his chair and gazed at her thoughtfully.

"Do you remember," he asked, "the day when I purchased you from your estimable father, during one of those periods of resting from banditry when he resided here? You were younger then – much younger. So also was I."

"You are no older now than a man should be who has attained his prime," she said, and waited.

"There was the usual moon that night – the moon which younger men than I do not fully value. I remember the journey at night (for we took a risk, did we not?) and the strange shadows on the banks of the river. There were shadows, too, where the moon cast them, the shadows of your breasts on your soft skin, the shadows . . . ."

Lien Fa let him be lyrical. She also remembered that journey, but her memory was better than the memory of Tung Lai Luk, for she recalled that it had poured with rain on that particular night, and the moon had not appeared once. Yet she said nothing of this, counting his imagination to his credit where the memory itself was very much on the other side of the ledger.

" I remember," said Lien Fa, letting the tip of her little finger caress the back of his neck, " as if it were yesterday."

" I intend to move south," said Tung Lai Luk. " To the British Colony of Hong Kong. Such money as I have been able to save without my wife's knowledge is already banked there."

Still the girl at the head of his chair sat silent. She was fanning him now.

" I cannot go to Hong Kong alone," said Tung Lai Luk.

" It would be unwise for you to do so," she answered. " For if you went alone, who would look after your clothes ? I will go and pack your small luggage, as well as my own. We could hire a boat and go down the river at night, as we did once before, long ago. . . ."

She did not tell him that her luggage had actually been packed for the last twelve hours, for men do not like discovering that their proposals are expected.

Chapter XXXI

YOU AGAIN?

Kung Hiao Ling led the party from the river bank. Beside him, Yang Fei pointed out the path along the raised banks between the paddy-fields towards the house where a light twinkled ahead of them.

"To return home is delightful, is it not?" the descendant of Confucius smiled at her. "Even to one who has been promised a post in the detective force of the city of Kwei Sek? It is a pity that Tung Lai Luk and the girl Lien Fa elected to stay behind. They would have enjoyed seeing this family reunion."

"To return home," answered Yang Fei, "is a privilege granted only to those who have left home. It has been, as you have already told me, the subject of innumerable poems and the inspiration of countless noble deeds. And yet – I do not know whether my father will welcome me as I should wish to be welcomed. Have a care, sir, at the corner of this field, for there used to be a muddy place. . . . I hope that my father will welcome me."

Ming So, slightly in the rear, was remembering the very similar paths between paddy-fields in his own village, and he felt just a little jealous of Yang Fei as he walked with the ex-bandit Lien Wo towards the lighted house ahead of them.

The party reached the door at last, and Kung Hiao Ling knocked sharply. Instantly all noises in the house were stilled, and after an interval a woman's voice called : " There is no hospitality in this house for travellers who come in the dusk."

Then Yang Fei cried : " Mother ! Open the door to my friends."

" What girl is calling me ' Mother ' ? " grumbled the voice. " I have but one more daughter besides those who are with me here, and she is no longer my daughter, for she was sold one moon ago to a merchant from the city. So depart and leave us in peace."

" This is indeed your daughter," called Yang Fei. " And with me are Kung Hiao Ling, the literary man, and Lien Wo, and a small boy, Ming So. We come to greet you."

" Not so much of the small boy," muttered Ming So, as those within seemed still to hesitate. " You at any rate ought to remember, Yang Fei, that I am not so small as your speech would make out. But your mother is a long time in opening the door."

He raised his voice and shouted.

" Ho, within there ! Open the door, for a shut door is shut only on such as should be concealed."

From within they heard a shrill cry.

" Ah, Ming So ! Come quickly, for these people have tied me up, and as for my mistress, whose name is Pak, they are . . ." Her voice subsided as a hand was held over the mouth of Pai Mei.

"It is Ah Mei, my sweetheart!" cried Ming. "Let us break down the door."

Lien Wo seized a large stone lying by the door and hurled it at the lock. This splintered, and the door swung open.

"I have no use for words, where deeds will suffice," said Lien Wo, as he entered complacently.

The family of Yang was drawn up at the other side of the room. Kung Hiao Ling put the ex-bandit behind him with a sweep of his arm.

"For this intrusion I must beg pardon," he said, and at the cultured, level tone of his voice the old woman Yang cried: "Ai-ah, it is a man who speaks poetry instead of words!" But he continued: "Our precipitate action in forcing an entrance here is explained, though not excused, by the cry of our young friend here" – he indicated Ming So – "when he heard the voice of the small girl with whom, I observe, he is now engaged. The real purpose of our visit was to bring back to you – if you want her – the girl Yang Fei, who was sold a while ago to a certain Tung Lai Luk, of the city of Kwei Sek. I may observe that your maternal delight at her return need not be tempered by the fear of having another mouth to feed, for she has obtained lucrative employment in the city."

Yang Fei had gone towards her mother. There was no demonstration about it, before all these strangers, for Yang Fei had passed the light-hearted age of Ming So and the little girl Pai Mei, now sitting side by side like a pair of love-birds, backs to the wall. And Yang Fei's mother, apart from her own lifelong habit of self-control, had other matters than rejoicing on her mind.

"I am glad to see my daughter, and more than glad to hear that she has a post which will support her and leave some money over for her family. For since the death of my husband I fear that our life here is very far from secure."

"I offer my own sorrow," replied Kung Hiao Ling, "for your unfortunate loss. It is perhaps presumptuous to enquire how events turned out in this way."

The old woman looked at her sons, then back at Kung Hiao Ling.

"I think that we should do best to tell this scholarly man the truth," she said. "After all, we have done no wrong greater than she did to us, when she killed my husband."

Lien Wo strode forward. He disliked words when actions would serve. "There is mystery here," he said, "and mystery is an unsatisfactory bedfellow." His hand moved to the latch of the bedroom door. "I propose to enter this door," he said, "because, all the time that my honourable friend Kung has been speaking I have been watching the stream of blood which has been trickling under it." He opened the door and went in.

The old woman wrung her hands. "She had a weapon – a revolver – and we intended to kill her, saying that it was in defence of our own lives. But, before we could do so, she had shot herself. Ah, if I could have got my hands to her ! "

Then Lien Wo came out of the bedroom, bearing a black, shiny box, which he opened on the floor in the middle of the room. " Bearer bonds, bank-notes, and jewellery," he said. " A small fortune."

Kung Hiao Ling interposed. " The bonds," he said, " belonged to Loo Heng, the Minister of Public Works of Kwei Sek, lately drowned owing to the agency of this woman, with whom he had intended to go to Hong Kong, where, in the British courts, Chinese justice does not extend. The notes and the jewellery are doubtless the property of the dead woman's husband, Tung Lai Luk, who will probably provide for the future of the family of Yang, as he is bound to do by our law, being responsible for the misdeeds of his wife. We shall see to that. For the rest . . ."

There was suddenly a thunderous knocking on the door of the building, which had swung to. Now it opened, to admit Po Feng Hsi, Chief of Police of Kwei Sek, and a posse of Chinese police.

" At last ! " he cried as he entered. " Why ! You here, Kung ? You are always anticipating me. Where is the woman Tung Nan Tsz, whom we seek ? "

Lien Wo, with a bow, indicated the bedroom and closed the black box with a click, handing it to Kung Hiao Ling. " You had better take charge," he said.

" We all know the haphazard methods of the police, and I, for one, would rather trust a literary man."

" Some of that money belongs to me," piped up Pai Mei. " The evil woman has not paid me for my services."

Po Feng Hsi returned from the inner room. " We must hold an enquiry, here and now," he said.

Kung yawned ostentatiously, and Ming So slipped out into the darkness with Pai Mei. He had several things to tell her.

.　　.　　.　　.　　.　　.　　.　　.

Ming So, who had gone into the house to see how the enquiry was proceeding, returned to find Yang Fei and Pai Mei rolling about on the ground in the dark. From sundry gasps and grunts he deduced that they were neither seeking some lost object nor suffering from an internal and painful complaint, but simply fighting.

He watched them, so far as the almost non-existent light permitted, and then interposed : " It is unfitting thus for girls to emulate the stronger sex ! The place of women, my uncle has often told me, is in bed. If women fought thus in bed . . ." He left unfinished the picture which his words conjured up. The two had ceased fighting now.

" She is a cat, the daughter of a cat, and a stealer of other girls' men ! " cried Pai Mei.

Yang Fei retorted : " I would rather be a cat than a monkey. And as for men – I desire nothing more of men. I have known them under various circumstances. . . ."

Ming So laughed. " In the matter of personal histories I beg of you not to be detailed," he said. " If circumstances threw a boy and a girl together, should the boy or the girl be blamed ? And as for you, Pai Mei, I can see, even in this darkness, that you have torn those black trousers which I remember your father buying for you. I think that the needle is more your weapon than the tongue – or finger-nails."

Yang Fei made the motion of spitting.

" Men are useless," she cried. " I want no more of them. Henceforth, in the detective service of Kwei Sek, I hope to expose and punish some of their baser actions. Not that you, Ming So, ever did anything which I might regret. But that was entirely because you could not – for no nobler reason."

" Cat ! " cried Pai Mei, returning to the assault.

Ming So shrugged his shoulders and went back indoors again to listen to his friend Kung Hiao Ling. If girls must fight, there was no need for men to witness the disgusting spectacle, he reflected.

" May I," asked Kung, as the boy entered, " constitute myself what I imagine you would call counsel for the family of Yang ? " He moved to the table where the Chief of Police was taking notes.

The Chief of Police sighed. " Is it not enough to have had you forestall me in arriving here ? " he demanded. "Would it be too much to ask of you to explain by what process of reasoning you managed to locate the missing woman Tung Nan Tsz? For I, by a series of complicated calculations, assisted by my staff, succeeded in ascertaining by mathematics the precise whereabouts of the place where she must be, only to find you here before us."

Kung smiled. "The boy Ming So will tell you, if you ask him, that I suggested this journey in order to restore the girl Yang Fei to the family from which she had been illegally taken away. I had been reading the poems of Li Po, you see, and came on the passage :

> *The nightjar wails its absent mate,*
> *And Youth grows old amongst the hills.*

Clearly, my duty was to see about the return of Yang Fei to her family."

Po Feng Hsi shook his head. "You are never willing to explain to me," he said. "Ah, well, keep to yourself the secret of your methods. As to your desire to act as counsel for the family, I have had sufficient acquaintance with the methods which I have mentioned, and with your literary abilities, to know by now that I shall be wise to agree. I suppose that entails a speech."

"It does," Kung began. "It appears to me, from what we already knew and from what you have discovered, that this woman, Tung Nan Tsz, pursued a course of action which we can enumerate thus." He ticked off the points on his fingers. " She put the girl Yang in a coffin and put the coffin aboard the motor-boat which her men had already stolen. Your motor-boat, Po ! " He smiled, and the other shifted uneasily in his seat. " The next action of this motor-boat was to take aboard a box containing papers – this box. Presumably the box and its contents were the property of Loo Heng, the Minister of Public Works, who has since been found drowned in the estuary of Kwei Sek River. You agree ? "

" Yes and no. But pray proceed."

Kung prepared to tick off another finger. " The woman, her two men, and the money in this box proceeded upstream, past your sleeping guards in the police station at Nam Pa. . . ."

" That is an unjustifiable statement," the Chief of Police interjected. " The officials of the police station had no reason and no right to stop the motor-boat."

" Perhaps not, O paragon of efficiency. Yet he would be a bold man who asserted that your policemen were not asleep. In any case, the point is immaterial. The motor-boat reaches the bank near the house of the hospitable Lien Wo, at the time appointed when this Lien Wo originally, a moon past, removed Tung Lai Luk from his boat on his passage downstream with the boy Ming So, his nephew."

" You are producing a very satisfactory analysis

of my notes," said Po Feng Hsi, "but I do not see wherein this is a speech for the family of Yang."

" No ? " Kung's voice was full of laughter. " Then I will proceed. The woman and her two men escape from us – a regrettable piece of work, that – and vanish in the motor-boat. The next scene is on the river bank near this house, where the small girl, Pai Mei, sits weeping because the money which she took from her mistress has been stolen, and she sees no means of reaching the city of Kwei Sek, where the boy, Ming So, seems to exercise a peculiar fascination for her.

" It is sad to picture the child, homeless, money-less, foodless, sitting thus on the river bank, sobbing her heart out. I think that a poem might be written about it, entitled ' The Nightjar in the River Reeds.' You would not imagine, to look at her now, that she could be the subject for such a poem. But to return. . . ."

" Good ! " interjected the Chief of Police.

Kung took no notice of him. " To return to our problem. She sees, down-river, a motor-boat. She sees the death of Yang Foo, the murder of the two men, and the sinking of the motor-boat. Yet con-sider the presence of mind of this child ! She sits there, still sobbing, and gives no clue to the wicked woman Tung Nan Tsz that she has seen what she has seen. She tells neither Tung Nan Tsz nor the Yang family. What wisdom ! For had she told, she would not be here now, in all probability, playing at love-birds with Ming So."

" Love-birds are wiser than more lonely birds," interjected Ming So suddenly, for he was affronted. " Besides, they make little noise."

" Thus all came to its appointed end," went on Kung. " The wicked woman plans to disappear. She did not even tell the little girl her real name, but gave the name of Mistress Pak. Does not ' Pak ' mean ' white,' which is both the symbol for purity and for death – a most suitable colour for her to choose ? "

" All which you say has the semblance of reality," answered the Chief of Police. " Still. . . ."

" But " – and Kung Hiao Ling here assumed an air of innocence – " there is one flaw in all this. The dead woman has been identified by Yang Fei, in whose interest it was to identify her as Tung Nan Tsz in order to excuse the woman's otherwise inexplicable death, here in her mother's house. But, under Chinese law, a body must be identified by a disinterested party. She was not disinterested – the very opposite. You yourself, Po Feng Hsi, would not be prepared to identify the somewhat untidy corpse in the next room as the Tung Nan Tsz who sat in your office during the previous enquiry into the death of Loo Heng. Consider – one woman amongst all the many whom you meet. No – I thought you would not identify her on oath. I only make the point as an academic one, but I feel that further identification by someone else, possibly by the woman's husband or those who knew her, is desirable. Who knows that this body is not just some common bandit, who desired to rob the Yang family and adopted this way of gaining entrance? It would be an amazing coincidence, but it needs proof."

" You are, I think," countered Po Feng Hsi, " making much of little. But since our idea of justice is what it is, and since, as you point out, identification must be carried out by a disinterested party, I fear that we must take the woman's body downstream with us, so that her husband or some other may say whether this is the body of Tung Nan Tsz or of some other bandit woman who happened to be here on our arrival."

Kung bowed. " That was what I intended to convey to you," he said. " I do not think that I shall accompany you, since I have other business to arrange. What is your intention with regard to the family of Yang? "

The Chief of Police explained : " I shall leave them here, with a guard. I shall do so for two reasons, which I trust you will recognise as valid – first, that I cannot be bothered taking all these women with me ; and, second, that someone must be left to do the necessary work on the farm. If one is left, why not all? For a guard would be necessary in any case."

" Your reasons seem as good as your actions," said Kung Hiao Ling, having got what he wanted.

Chapter XXXII

SECOND ATTEMPT

TUNG LAI LUK leaned back in his chair on the passenger deck of the S.S. *Mo Kam Fai*. Beside him sat Lien Fa, sewing busily.

" The day is finer than your industry deserves," he said complacently, " for such occupations as sewing are best fitted for a day whereon a looker out of a window sees rain, pouring rain, drawing slanting lines down the window, whilst the wind bends to their roots the bamboos which his garden should possess. But now the sun shines. It is no time for sewing."

Lien Fa did not raise her eyes from her work. " If we women chose only wet days for our needlework," she observed, " you men would complain of us as butterflies."

He groaned aloud. " Ah Fa, you remind me painfully sometimes of my other wife, which is unwise of you. She is by now, I trust, expiating her crimes as a result of the uncanny penetration of Po Feng Hsi, the Chief of Police. I remember that she used to make just the same sort of remark about men. Before she took to men as a hobby, that is."

Lien Fa poised her needle. " She was a very evil woman," she said, without a blush. " But it was her wickedness which sent you to me, so that I should be thankful for that wickedness."

"I am not asking" – and the voice of Tung Lai Luk was the voice of one who has unlocked the door to laughter – "I am not asking what peculiar sins of hers were known to you. I have had enough of questioning of motives and comparison of characters. Suffice it that I have a sufficiency of money in the bank in Hong Kong to save me from the necessity of working, so that I shall be able to devote enough time to you, Ah Fa, to keep you occupied."

She made a *moue*. "Virtue begets virtue," she said, "and living with you should be enough for any woman. No doubt you will not let me languish of boredom. Husbands who allow their wives to languish thus have only themselves to thank. But, in any case, she was a very evil woman. I do not desire to speak further of her. Unless" – she added – "you insist on it. Then I can but be dutiful."

He rose to his feet and balanced himself as the boat rolled.

"No," he said, "I do not so desire. For the sun shines, and the waves reflect the light of the sun, and I can stand thus and stretch my limbs in the knowledge that I am no longer a business man."

"I do not know that you ought to give up business altogether," she said innocently. "But tell me, are the shops pleasant in Hong Kong? I have heard much talk of them. My late mistress used to talk about the Hong Kong shops to Loo Heng, whom she drowned, and to Loo Ching, whom she killed another way. I must confess that shops have always had a peculiar attraction for me."

But Tung Lai Luk was not listening to her. " To be free ! " he cried to the wind. " To have no further care for money, for an erring wife with murderous leanings, for a nephew whose one thought is of his belly. Oh, that boy ! "

" He was very young," replied Lien Fa, remembering. " Like a little skinned rabbit in the electric light, I remember. It used to amuse Loo Ching very much. Ah, well, such things are not good to think about too deeply."

" I am sorry about your father," said Tung, sitting down again. " He has gained nothing from his deals, either with my wife or with my unworthy self."

" On the contrary," the girl returned demurely, " he has gained two things."

" What may they be ? " enquired her lord and master.

" He has gained a thousand dollars, in spite of the honourable Kung's discovery that the notes were forgeries. Of course, I do not know whence your late wife obtained them, but I do know that my father, when he had recovered from his first rage, examined them carefully and decided that what was good enough to deceive him was good enough to deceive others. So that is not so bad. Also, since I often used to borrow money from him with no intention of repaying it, he has lost a certain amount of avoidable expense."

" Mm ! Yes," Tung Lai Luk agreed somewhat dubiously. " I shall sleep now. You can go on with your sewing."

" I do hope," thought Lien Fa, as she stitched, " that he will not prove either too loving or too keen-sighted. Both failings are apt to be awkward." She paused for a moment in her sewing, then went on again. The second mate, a rather handsome northerner, had passed her on his way to the chart-room.

When she looked up an instant later, the second mate was looking back.

Chapter XXXIII

TALE OF A HAT

KUNG HIAO LING had chartered, amidst great excitement, the only two carrying-chairs in Ch'ang Sui. That thus devehicled village had now been left far behind, and the two chairs bounced steadily along the road to Ha Foo. Kung himself sat placidly smoking in one chair, pondering on some abstruse and literary matter. From the second chair came at intervals small squeals and gurgles, so that the bearers, sweating as they were, muttered remarks about love-birds.

" It is more kind of the gods than we deserve," sighed Pai Mei in her ecstasy.

" What is this talk of gods ? " came Ming So's reply, as he snuggled his arm protectingly round her. " Praise rather the acumen, the penetration, the clearsightedness, of men such as Kung Hiao Ling, who sits smoking in the other chair, or of myself, who have – the two of us – brought justice where crime was before, have turned a tragedy into a comedy. I will not say farce."

" What is justice ? " the little girl asked, not because she wanted to know, but because Ming So was bound to talk, in any event, and it would be as well if she gave him a subject.

" Justice ? Why, O uneducated one, justice is

Qw

what makes possible the business of the world."

" I thought that money made possible the business of the world," said Pai Mei.

" Money and justice sleep in the same bed," he replied, conscious of the epigram.

" Oh ! " was all that she could manage, for just at that moment he squeezed her again. . . .

" Fools and swallows twitter," grunted Kung Hiao Ling, from the other chair.

.   .   .   .

Twenty *li*, like twenty of anything else, come to an end. The bearers threaded their way along the rough road between the paddy-fields, past the cottage of the leather-worker, over the humped bridge, out at the far side of the village, and finally set their burdens down a stone's throw short of Ming Nai's cottage.

" To approach on foot is more considerate than to drown with the creak of shafts the faint sighing of what wind there is, as it moves, restless, round the devil-corners of your mother's house," said Kung. " Therefore the coolies will follow, with our insignificant baggage, some little way in the rear. You, Ming So, will walk slightly behind me, on my left. Behind you this female twitterer will walk, as becomes the woman she is not yet. Advance ! "

Ming Nai opened the door of the cottage. Her quick eyes took in the unknown Kung, the remembered Ming So, the regrettable Pai Mei. But she stood before the man, remaining with eyes downcast, waiting his words.

" Once, at the Eastern Gate, a girl stood watching the horsemen file past to the city," he began, in words chosen like tiles for a mosaic.

Ming Nai raised her eyes diffidently, for even cynics must know that a literary man is more than other men.

" A girl so stood," she replied, " and the dust rose from the horses' hoofs as the horsemen passed."

" Of these horsemen one, as his mount proved restless, dropped his cap." Kung spoke still in the same chosen words. " The girl picked up this cap and, graceful as willow in spring breeze, came forward and returned it to the rider."

" Their hands almost touched," she said. " But . . ."

" But ? "

" But the horsemen rode on." She lowered her eyes again.

" Horsemen return in chairs," said Kung Hiao Ling. " May we enter your house ? "

She bowed and moved backwards into the cottage. The philosopher also bowed. Then he turned to the children.

" Take this money," he said, " and proceed in the chairs to the village food-shop. Once there, order from the surprised tradesman sufficient for a comfortable meal for us four, and also a modicum for the coolies who have so uncomplainingly transported us.

So – go ! " He turned again and entered after Ming Nai.

" There is much to say," he observed, " before the return of the two children. It would therefore be as well to start now. But, before other words are spoken, may I ask you to name the amount which the girl took from your secret store, so that I may replace it before her return ? I wish to see whether that sprightly young mind reacts to surprise. No – do not question or object. Tell me the amount."

Ming Nai did so, and Kung Hiao Ling, counting out notes for the missing money, placed them in the drawer which Ming Nai showed to him. " Now we can talk," he said. " Ceremony is all very well in its place, but its place is not here. Let us be seated, that I may tell you all that has happened, and the changed circumstances which have arisen since a horseman dropped his cap and a girl picked it up and returned it to him."

.   .   .   .

It was definitely amusing, the boy Ming So reflected, to sit eating peanuts and watch the ball of intelligence tossed backwards and forwards by his mother and Kung Hiao Ling, as they remembered epigrams and aphorisms from the classics to cover every subject on which they conversed. And yet he felt, too, that the subjects in question were somehow restricted to one subject, and that a subject on which he and Pai Mei had not in the past been backward to chatter.

" But," his mother would say, " the fox that has once been trapped fears the trap, the wounded bird avoids the neighbourhood of archers."

At this Kung would smile. " The fox is incapable, being an animal of limited intelligence, of distinguishing between the former trap and the present estimable offer of a fox-burrow. The bird, wounded in the past by an unworthy archer, is apt to regard even an unarmed man as dangerous. The argument is prone to follow the emotions rather than the reason, if those emotions have been aroused. Not that emotion, in itself, is a bad thing. . . . "

" For a woman," Ming Nai retorted, " emotion and instinct are safeguards against the cold reason of men. Their support of a case makes it invulnerable, their opposition takes from beneath it the ladder of possibility."

" Yet reflect," Kung said, " on those very emotions to which you thus appeal. Do you not read them in the light of a fear that is dead and done with ? Look them squarely in the face. Admit that you are not unattracted, really, by my unconventional offer. Abandon the prejudice born of the sorrow of the past years, and admit that you are not as hostile to the idea as you would make out. After all, our childish memories should not be wholly disregarded, and the girl who once picked up a horseman's cap should not, now, be the woman who tramples on that cap."

Ming Nai smiled. " Oh, yes, you can twist words

as no one else can. I grant you that. You can paint
a pigsty into a palace. You can make the archer's
arrow appear the harmless wand of the water-
diviner. Oh, yes, it is easy to talk."

Kung raised his hands to his ears. "What would
you?" he demanded. "The Master says: *If
language is lucid, that is enough,* and I cannot accept
blame for my ability to put my thoughts into words.
For consider that, if men were unable to express
their ideas, they would be no better than the beasts."

"To take a case which is too extreme convinces
not even yourself," she replied. "But, at any rate,
should not you consider the tradition which our
nation has built up round the sayings of your great
ancestor, Confucius? You know that no follower
of his teaching approves of a widow exchanging her
own roof-tree for another."

"You do not believe in tradition," he returned.

"No, but you do. It would not look well if the
Master's descendant set at naught the Master's
teaching."

"I will answer that in two different ways," said
Kung. "The first way is by pointing out that my
ancestor himself never put forward any such pro-
hibition as you have mentioned. I should therefore
be doing well in showing that I, at least, do not
subscribe to the later accretions which now dis-
figure his theories of life. The second way of
answering you is to say that, even if such behaviour
were frowned on by tradition, man is his own

master, and that it would be folly to allow a code to become a ritual, to turn a recipe for cooking into the law of a nation. You cook for pleasure and comfort : you govern a nation for the nation's prosperity. Neither should interfere with a free man's right to his own free will. Further, you need not change your roof-tree, as you said, for I like this village as well as most, and I think that I might write poems here. . . . "

The little girl Pai Mei tugged at Ming So's sleeve.

" Come away," she said. " They waste words."

Chapter XXXIV

IN ACCORDANCE WITH THE CRIMINAL CODE

Po Feng Hsi laid down his brush and read through his report of the case of Tung Nan Tsz as far as he had written it. Then, taking up the brush again and damping it with precisely the correct amount of ink from the slab, he proceeded.

" The body of the woman could not be identified at Nam Pa, owing to the departure of the husband, Tung Lai Luk, with the girl Lien Fa for an unknown destination. On arrival at Kwei Sek the body was already showing signs of a more than incipient decay, but identification was achieved through four girls from the Government silk factory, who gladly came to view the body, saying that they were gratified to see the end of their former employer.

" The above-mentioned departure of Tung Lai Luk and the girl Lien Fa had, I suspect, been anticipated by the illustrious Kung Hiao Ling, who had, however, made no attempt to stop the elopement. When questioned, Kung will probably reply that Tung deserved better luck with his second wife, and that he is, seemingly, not buying unsampled goods.

" In order to conclude the case in accordance with the Criminal Code, it was needful to arrange for the future of the family of Yang, who, owing to the death of the aged fish-winner ('bread-winner' would be incorrect), were now without visible means of obtaining rice.

" This difficulty will be overcome by the sale of the jewellery found in the possession of the dead woman, and the investment of the proceeds in Salt Loan. The bearer bonds found in her box have been handed over to the family of the late Loo Heng, after due confirmation had been obtained that these bonds were in the possession of Loo Heng when he left his house and was later found, drowned, in the harbour.

" I have described this case in more detail than might have been expected, because at every step the literary man, Kung Hiao Ling, has in some way altered the sequence and the setting of facts by his habit of acting on the strength of such things as poetry or the direction of the wind. Had I not thus set down my own account, those hearing of it from Kung or his friends might have suspected in the police of the province an accession of that poetical and unpractical spirit which was the glory of the T'ang Dynasty, but seems out of place in the agents of the law in Republican China.

" He signs this who wrote it.

" Po Feng Hsi."

The Chief of Police again laid down his brush with a profound sigh and picked up the volume of the poems of Li Po which he had lately borrowed from his friend Kung, while the latter was away from his rooms.

> *Is it dew makes the jade threshold glisten –*
> *   Just dew ?*
> *Or do thresholds weep, as they listen*
> *   For you ?*

He closed the book again. " That is great poetry," he observed to nobody in particular. Then he struck the gong at his side. To the constable who entered, he said : " Send to me the new girl detective, Yang Fei. I fancy that, if she has a mind to, she may be able to enlighten me on one of the poems of the great Li Po, a poem which I find a little obscure."

" She has gone out," replied the constable, smiling behind his hand, for it was already rather a joke in the station about the Chief of Police and his romantic attachment for his new detective. " The little girl who had no name is sweeping out her room, and told me that at the time of preparing for the evening meal she would be in the restaurant of the ' Seven Heavenly Dishes,' engaged on police business, doubtless, although the little girl whom she brought from ' The Happy Heart ' did not tell me this."

" You talk too much," said Po Feng Hsi, reaching (with another sigh) for his street coat.

Chapter XXXV

HANGING WATERS

The pool below the waterfall reflected the faint skyline of the fringing trees on the far side. To-night there was no moon whatever, but the stars hung only just out of reach in the low sky. Towards the fall itself the mirrored images of the stars and of the skyline were lost in ripples – as the children looked farther, towards the remote, shallower end, warm stars took their being, first in swaying streaks of gold, then in curious, small ellipses, and finally in steadier, only slightly swaying points.

The sibilant purr of the fall sounded continuously, like a background of thoughts which cannot be denied entrance to the conscious mind.

" It is very dark," complained Pai Mei, as she stood there holding Ming So's arm. " I can hardly see my feet."

" What need is there for a light ? " he demanded. " We are older now, if only a little, and now we know more of the world. At least, I do. Therefore I rely less on bright lights, which only illuminate the surface of things."

" It is not very cold," said her voice hopefully.

" No – it is not very cold. But what do you mean by that observation ? For surely you are not given overmuch to noticing the temperature or the other

251

ways in which Nature manifests itself? There lies behind your remark some further remark, which you presumably have not courage to utter."

She did not answer this directly. Instead she said : " If I stretched out my hand, I could pick one of the stars, like a ripe golden plum." Then she sighed. " And there would be one less star in the sky. The last time that I came here, I went behind the hanging waters of the fall and there were wonderful things there – an old man who was blind, with an otter which brought him fish for food. He told me of my past and of my future, but, because I was foolish and a little afraid, I had told him I was a boy. So I saw, instead of my own, the past and future of Ming So."

" *Study of the supernatural is injurious indeed*," replied Ming So, quoting Confucius. " And I think that you should have given some other name than mine, because . . . "

But she took no heed of what he was saying. " He showed me the room in the city of Kwei Sek, where that woman Yang Fei pillowed your head on her knees. She is indeed a polecat, and the daughter of a polecat, for neither of you had any clothes on."

" That was a lamentable occurrence, and none of my seeking," answered the boy.

" He also showed me the future, round a camp fire on the river bank. That has already happened, I suppose."

" It has," he replied.

" Then let us go and see him now."

" Very well," said Ming So. " We must be careful not to lose our clothes, because it is very dark. I shall hang mine on this bush, here."

" And I on this," Pai Mei replied, doing so.

The water was, as one might expect, chilly for the first moment, but as the two waded farther into the water the chill seemed to pass.

" How does he see in the cave ? " Ming So asked.

" Foolish ! Did I not say that he was blind ? Should I have gone into the cave, I, with no clothes at all, if he had not been blind ? But there is flint and steel and tinder for making a fire on which to cook fish which the otter brings, so we could. . . ."

" I am anxious to see this man. It seems to me that it would be convenient thus to foreknow the future. Much money might be made thereby in the city."

" It is pleasant to have money," said Pai Mei, as if it were a very small matter. " This waterfall takes the breath away, but just behind it is a shelf of rock, to which it is necessary to climb. Will you lift me up ? For last time I scratched my knee."

" Girls are awkward things," he answered. " For ever needing assistance from man. But I will do as you say." He put his head through the veil of water, and gasped : " Ai-ah ! But I can see nothing whatever now."

Her voice beside him whispered : " Can you not put one leg up, as if you were going to climb ? Then I can step on it, like a ladder."

" There is a convenient rock here," he observed.
" Thus. Now, hold my shoulder. Give me your
foot. There. Now climb." He reflected that there
was no real reason for her little toes to wriggle as he
held her round the hips, standing on his bent
thigh. " Go on : climb up." He heard the little
wet squelch as her body reached the stone floor of
the cave, and promptly pushed the rest of her after
it. " Now find the flint and steel, for I cannot see
at all."

After an interval he saw first one spark, then a
shower. For an instant her little, narrow face was
outlined, then only the vision persisted. Again she
struck flint on steel.

" It is no use," she cried petulantly. " The tinder
is damp. And there is no one in the cave. Come :
climb up."

But as the boy pulled himself out from the water
behind him and lay on the stone floor, the spark fell
on a drier part of the tinder, and she coaxed the tiny
flame into life and lit one of the rush torches stuck
in a crack of the rock wall. The flickering, yellow
glare made them both blink.

" And, now that you have brought me here, what
is to be done ? " queried Ming So. " I wonder
where the old man has gone. Ai-ah ! You are not
nearly as old as the girl Yang Fei ! Is there another
passage into this cave ? "

She did not reply, but led the way, holding the
torch above her head. They passed along a tunnel,

rising under their feet, a tunnel which became
narrower and lower, so that finally, stooping, they
emerged round the side of a vast boulder into the
open air, under the same low, yellow stars. But now
the surrounding trees made them feel as if they were
viewing the sky from the bottom of a pit : the space
was a small garden, whose blooms showed only of a
lighter grey in the yellow glare of the torch.

" It is a garden ! " cried Ming So, with surprise
in his voice.

" When we are married, we shall live here," the
girl asserted in the manner of wives who plan.
" But where can the old man be ? "

" There never was an old man," he told her. " It
was one of the spirits of the hills, with whom your
father, Pai Kwat, has dealings."

" That cannot be, for I saw him with my own eyes,
and heard with my own ears the story of your
carryings-on with the abominable girl Yang Fei.
No : he was a real man. But he was very old, and I
expect that he has gone away to die. Old men do
that."

" It is a sad thought," said Ming So, and he softly
hummed the burial song, chanted over the graves of
common men.

> " *Whose is the graveyard ?*
> *Ghosts crowd within it,*
> *Wise with the unwise,*
> *Death's King their master –*
> *Man's doom delays not.*"

He ceased humming. "Ai-ah, it is a sad thought. But we are young, and it is foolish to talk of death when you are young. Shall we go back now?"

"I suppose so," agreed the girl dreamily. "We could take some of these flowers back with us into the cave, to hang on the walls. There are rugs there already – the rugs on which the old man used to sit."

They returned through the rock passage, and as they sat down on the pile of rugs the otter came and laid a fish at their feet, biting neatly at the back of the head, so that the movement of the fish became tiny tremors of the fins.

"He mistakes me for the old man of whom you were telling me," said Ming So with a smile. "Light a fresh torch, for I have had enough of sitting in the dark with a girl."

"Kung and your mother will marry," she said as she rose and went to the store of torches. "What is this marriage?"

"It is very like sitting alone in the dark with a girl," chuckled Ming So, as she returned to his side on the pile of rugs. He chuckled to conceal the manner in which his teeth wanted to chatter, although he was not cold, and also the fact that he was very much afraid, just as he had been once before. . . .

THE END